BLACK IDOL

Lisa St Aubin de Terán was born in London in 1953. At the age of sixteen she left James Allen's Girls' School to marry. She and her exiled Venezuelan husband travelled for two years in Italy before returning to his family home in the Andes. After seven years, during which she managed her husband's sugar plantation and avocado farm, she came back to England with her daughter. Lisa St Aubin de Terán is the author of *Keepers of the House*, winner of the Somerset Maugham Award in 1983, *The Slow Train to Milan*, winner of the John Llewelyn Rhys Memorial Prize for 1983, *The Tiger*, and *The Bay of Silence* which is also available in Pavanne.

Also by
Lisa St Aubin de Terán in Pavanne
The Bay of Silence

BLACK IDOL

Lisa St Aubin de Terán

published by Pan Books
in association with Jonathan Cape

First published in Great Britain 1987 by Jonathan Cape Ltd
This edition published 1988 by Pan Books Ltd, Cavaye Place, London SW10 9PG
in association with Jonathan Cape Ltd
9 8 7 6 5 4 3 2 1
© Lisa St Aubin de Terán
ISBN 0 330 30335 X

Printed and bound in Great Britain by
Cox & Wyman Ltd, Reading

For Iseult

Author's Note

In 1979 I went to New York and stayed at the Hôtel des Artistes. It was then that I first heard the name of Harry Crosby, and of his loves and life. This book grew out of that time and place. It begins in the Hôtel des Artistes, with its view of the Chrysler Building, in 1929, when Harry Crosby was there with his mistress, Josephine.

Chronology

1898   Harry Crosby (Henry Grew Crosby) was born in Boston into a wealthy and influential banking family. His godfather and uncle was J. Pierpont Morgan Jr, the richest man in the world.

1908   Josephine Noyes Rotch was born in Boston into a distinguished family of Nantucket Quakers.

1911   Harry attends St Mark's School, Southborough, near Boston.

1917   Harry graduates from St Mark's School in June. In July he sails for France as a volunteer for the American Field Service Ambulance Corps.

      22 November, Verdun – a shell destroys Harry's ambulance and seriously injures his friend Way (Spud) Spaulding. Harry escapes, miraculously unharmed.

1919   Harry is decorated and records his relief in a diary entry: 'Oh Boy!!!!!! Won the CROIX DE GUERRE. Thank God.'

      He returns to Boston, 'city of dreadful night'.

1920   Harry Crosby meets Mrs Richard Rogers Peabody

(née Mary Phelps Jacob) whom he eventually rechristens Caresse and marries.

1922   Harry follows Mrs Peabody to Paris. The tempestuous and newly divorced Mrs Peabody abandons Paris and Harry to return to America.

Harry proposes to 'Polly' Peabody by telegram and then sails to New York in hot pursuit. They marry in New York and return to France. Harry is employed by his uncle. He commutes to work each morning, rowing down the Seine in a red felucca.

1923   Harry resigns from the Morgan, Harjes & Co. Bank.

1923-5   The Crosbys live a life of decadence and romance. They gamble, buy a race horse, write poetry and Harry worships the sun. They travel in France, Italy and Spain.

1926   Josephine Rotch attends Bryn Mawr College. Harry and Caresse buy a whippet, Narcisse Noir, whose claws Harry gilds regularly.

The Crosbys meet Ernest Hemingway and Archibald MacLeish.

1927   Harry and Caresse found the Black Sun Press which will publish some of the finest works of the 1920s.

The Crosbys go to see the arrival of Charles Lindbergh's *Spirit of St Louis* in Paris. Harry's cousin, Walter Berry, dies.

1928   The Crosbys go to Egypt, Jerusalem, Turkey and Yugoslavia. Harry nearly dies from an overdose of hashish. He smokes opium (black idol).

1928   Josephine Rotch leaves Bryn Mawr to marry Albert Smith Bigelow. Before her marriage she goes to Europe to buy her trousseau.

1928 Harry inherits 8,000 rare books from his cousin Walter Berry. He gives them all away.

1929 In June Harry has a throat operation in Lausanne. Later the Crosbys travel to Venice.

In July Harry meets Josephine Rotch at the Lido. They fall in love. Josephine returns to America.

In August Harry meets Jonathan Cape, who wants to publish his journal (*Shadows of the Sun*).

In November Harry returns to America.

1929 Harry acquires a student pilot's licence and meets Hart Crane, whose poem 'The Bridge' he publishes at Black Sun Press.

Josephine Rotch and Albert Bigelow in Old Lyme, Connecticut. In November Harry receives a one-word radiogram from Josephine, his 'Fire Princess' : 'IMPATIENT'.

Early in December, Harry and Josephine stay together at the Hotel Book-Cadillac in Detroit. They sign in as Mr & Mrs Harry Crane. Harry introduces Josephine to black idol.

10 December, New York. Harry arranges to meet his wife and mother for tea at J. P. Morgan's house on Madison Avenue. In the evening they are to dine and go to the theatre with Hart Crane. On the same day Harry borrows Stanley Mortimer's studio in the Hôtel des Artistes where he meets with Josephine who is very drunk.

One

I've always been a dreamer, ever since I can remember. Before I even knew what love was, let alone sex; before I ever went to France, or even Bryn Mawr, I was a dreamer and a doer. I couldn't sit around sipping tea, waiting for things to happen. In Drearytown that can be a long wait. It can be for ever, never. So, sure, maybe I did shock a few people, but they really needed shocking. Most of all, though, I had dreams to follow; and I'd been dreaming long before I went to Venice, long before black idol, and long before I met you, Harry, the one and only Harry Crosby who was living a dream and making it come true.

You always wanted to be something you weren't, to have something or someone you hadn't got, and that took a lot of looking for sometimes. I mean, who didn't you have, and what? I guess you weren't a great poet though, and that's what you wanted more than anything. And Caresse? Your darling, ageing, large-breasted wife, Caresse? She wanted so much, she was like a neap tide dragging out your insides across constantly renewing shingle. She wanted to be someone too. To be famous, to do something. And Caresse Crosby invented a new kind of brassière – no wires, no supports. But where does that leave her now her own breasts have begun to wilt?

Everyone likes Caresse. Why should I pretend to like her

when you know I don't? She'll be as shocked as anyone. They'll all be shocked. Boston rocked to its foundations. Boston clammed up into that tight core we both came from. Boston made bitter with rage – or is it outrage – but still the same old Drearytown with its bright-eyed faces and its dull-tongued talk.

You'll be seen as the bad one, Harry, the instigator. I'm just a young girl, a June bride. Maybe a few of your old flames will mutter the blame on to me, say I'm mad, that I led you astray. But people have been calling me mad for nearly half my life. So I've traded in eleven years of insanity for something altogether more lasting here with you.

We will be one, Harry, not simply 'twins', mistaken for brother and sister. My past is gone. Whatever I remember seems to have reshaped itself around you. I want you for always. Not your always, an afternoon or a week if I'm lucky. Not your 'I'm with you now but I can't answer for later.'

So this is the beginning – a couple in love embarking on a journey together. It could have been our life together but it isn't, because I'm Josephine Bigelow, née Rotch, of Back Bay, Boston. Age twenty-two, the wild and beautiful wife of hockey-champion Albert. And then there's Caresse, and Caresse has got her claws into you. And we're all Bostonians, which means we can go so far and no farther. So it's a journey, not a life. It's not like that, the way it could have been, not any more.

I guess being together is all that matters. I've been so confused these last weeks. Half the time I haven't been able to see where I'm going – but it's not like that any more. I can see it clearly now, Harry. Only I feel so bitter, bitter and frustrated.

Just an hour ago, when the dark wind crept up out of the East River and over the aluminium plates of the Chrysler Building, and the heat began to dwindle, what little there was of it in the wind, and with the sun about to settle on to the pillow of the New Jersey oil-cracking plants we lay down together on top of the silk. And you took me into your arms, and we did what we always do, only not so well, Harry. Not as before with quite such an earth-shaking sense of the San Andreas fault opening, as it did oh so many times, watching the green light circle from the pylon on top of the Ritz, with you, Harry, feeling the secret flood of your golden semen. It had to be gold, Harry, in you it had to be gold overcoming my own withdrawal. But, Harry, supposing that then it had been as often, and not as today, only, a stale thing, and the reality had not to be mimed, a false quiver, an eye flutter, a tremor in the groin faked. Oh, Harry, forgive me, but that's how it was – yet if it had swooped, as usual, like the great eagle it used to be, and lifted me over the hill, sliding into valleys of singing thrushes, then I might have lain here at peace.

I've read that his whole life flashes past a drowning man as he goes under. I don't think that could happen to you, though, your life has been so full, you'd choke. I could help you, even make you see it all. 'The bewitching Josephine Rotch' could once more demonstrate her power, 'the wildcat Mrs Bigelow' throw another scene, get hysterical, have her way . . . but you know, Harry, it's not like that, not any more. It's just you and me, now, the way we wanted it to be, the way we planned it, right back in Venice; and there'll be no more scenes at all.

So, Harry, let's pretend it's still only three-thirty. We're laughing, talking, the bottle of Cutty Sark is only half empty, your story about Hart Crane half told. Why did you say it was not the right time? The dim orange ball cradled in the scaffolding of the Fuller Building, not yet over the hill, or sinking into the Ganges, where the old blind man you admired so much was carried every morning to see it rising and stayed, as if watching, his dark orbs turning to feel the heat, until it settled, setting, and he was carried away contented. Why did you say it was not yet time when I asked you, as I had to ask you, Harry?

You touched the sun tattooed on the sole of your foot, and

you poured more Scotch in the only clean glass. You went over and stared out as the old Indian man must have done, crinkling your eyes up, removing your eye-glasses the way you always do when you want to make love. You said it was too soon still, Harry, glancing at your watch, moving a book on the table beside the bed, waiting, making me wait, the way you always made me wait. Even in Venice. Even there, at the Lido. Even now, Harry.

Then it was time, later, it was nearly the right time, only two hours to sundown, and four hundred yards away in a house on Madison Avenue your mother was meeting your wife to have tea with J. Pierpont Morgan, your uncle, the great banker. He must be feeling very angry you haven't come, not knowing how busy you are with a girl on the ninth floor of the Hotel des Artistes on the other side of the Park, taking the first step along the road we've both chosen.

But the time, Harry, has got to be right. You always have to be sure of that. You might have done it there in the sleazy bar in Detroit, four days ago when we were out of our minds on black idol, drinking rum from a pair of broken teacups. You might have done it there, I know, one hand under my lace pretties over the soaking calyx of what you've learned to want with your tongue. One hand putting it there, out of sight under the silk, exciting me, making me want it more, want it then and there, the hot explosion breaking into the place where my unborn baby is now, Harry – you know she is.

Sure you care, Harry, but is that enough? Only everything is enough. You wanted to believe in another world, in another age, when our only love-child might have grown in my womb to the real daughter I swear she is for me now. And, yes, might have turned, even, been crowned, and slid like a great little *Cutty Sark* very slowly, and, yes, rather competently, between my greased thighs and into the sun. Your beautiful sun, Harry. Your daughter standing naked, arms wide in the shape of the Cross, born to be singed as black as your own back in the force of the sun.

14

That's what you wanted. I know you did, in another world. In another time, when the time was not so wrong. But it was always wrong. Meanwhile, only the catapulting into ever-increasing spirals of tension mattered. Only the headlong rush along the runway in the tottering biplane, up and into the air. Only the flood of speed in a Chrysler heading for the edge of the cliff, the risk, Harry, the special instant, the annihilation of trivia in a glaze of art, this was what made the difference.

Never mind, Harry, just be near me and I'll be all right. And be my mirror. After all, it's an age of mirrors, isn't it? You always said we lived in an age of mirrors. Well, they never told me that at Bryn Mawr. They never told me the mirrors would break in a jagger of shattering pieces over its granite walls. They never told me in eighteen months I'd be lying on a hard bed in a studio duplex three blocks from the Park, with my clinging skirt on and my shoes off. Lying with my grandmother's best long string of pearls around my neck, and a pair of silk stockings laddered up to the garters from straining my legs around the buttocks of a man wearing a double-breasted jacket from Brooks Brothers, and no trousers, and my mouth fixed in a sad Mona Lisa smile, and my hair mussed. No, they never told me that either.

How does it feel, Harry? How does it feel to be standing fully dressed now, except for your shoes, your fine polished lizardskin shoes, fitting a cigarette in your amber holder, and striking a match, and listening? How does it feel to be listening to your lonely girl lying back there on a bed a little untidily with her eyes glazed over? Her hands loose at her sides, her lips parted, but not really saying very much, in fact anything at all, or likely to, except for this endless monologue you can't help hearing inside your own head.

Now. Imagine a wire recorder, Harry, like something at Reuters, say, turning slowly, sucking down whatever I say now, whatever I think, even, a microphone over there above the window lifting the sounds out of my mouth. Pasting them down here beside the bed on the thin strip of tape on the reel, your own ideas, Harry, your own words thrown on the black screen which is all I have left to give you now. The reflecting surface of two hours, maybe, of intensities never to be forgotten, never believed, never understood.

Suppose the bottle of Scotch over there on the chest of drawers were to float over and into your hand, and you took a long pull, Harry. Suppose, too, there was opium in the room, and you lit a pipe, and smoked a while, and the alcohol and the black idol linked hands and made a man, or a demon, out of you – would you have the courage, Harry? Would you have the guts, as the English girls at school used to call it? – I wonder why, were they thinking about the twisting churn in their own bellies, Harry? Would you have the bare animal urge, to come over and settle yourself on the edge of the bed, and lay your hand on me?

Suppose, if you blew on your hands, you could make it all melt away – the big mirrors, the deal wardrobe, the reproduction of Picasso's 'Guitar Players' by the window, the plant stand, the row of books in the bookcase, the window itself, and the first-class etching of East Manhattan framed there with its orange lights, and its winter stars. Would you wish the deed away as well as the room? Would you wish me away too, Harry? So you could run away to the hotel and charm your rich uncle once more and try to block out the thought that I'll always be there in your mind's eye as I am now?

Use me, Harry. Draw the curtains in case some Indian stevedore on the scaffolding of the Fuller Tower should unsling his binoculars, three hundred feet in the sky, and focus a flashlight, and stare in and down at a wicked man pulling his trousers off and, for the second time that afternoon, stroking his ample foreskin with his itching fingers. Come over here and feel under my skirt for the twisting blackness of my stocking, and, yes, Harry, you could still do this. You could still lay your poor head in my lap, and lick. Lick me, Harry. Lick away the tension, the hatred, the fear and the need.

16

What brought you here and keeps you in this room, Harry? A dream, our dream. You can't leave, and how long can you sit by me or pace the floor? We've acted this out but it's not over yet. Before it is the right time you can look back. I can't seem to see myself except in relation to you now, Harry. You're my sun and I'm your Fire Princess – the only one who takes your dream seriously enough to make it real, Harry. Me, Harry – not Caresse nor any of the other wives you've borrowed – I'm here to see it through by your side. So let's look together, Harry, until the time is right.

Two

On the map it looks like a pair of ham-bones. Interlocking joints. That's what I thought when I folded open the old map in my Baedeker in the train. We were over the frontier by then, and I'd had my coffee, and a pair of rolls, and some orange juice and a cigarette, and I was back in the couchette on my own, the mist rolling away in the sun, the smoke laid out like a solid plume along the rocks, and then over fields, and in forty-five minutes the Orient Express, or the slip-coach as they called it, so I'd learned, would be reaching Venice.

Imagine me, Harry. Twenty years old, and as wild as they come, as wild as I am now, and alone, alone except for a pair of maroon leather suitcases and a hat-box, and a rolled frilly umbrella and some high-heeled shoes, alone except for my Baedeker and my dreams, on my way to the Queen of the Adriatic to get her help in buying my trousseau.

Paris was fine. Sure, I had most of what I needed, after hours in tiny scented shops, with tiny scented women bending over my shoulders, and soft pliable hands moulding lingerie to my waist. I was richer and poorer, both at once, less money still in the Chase Manhattan account my father had laid aside for my clothes, but endowed with a wealth of magnificent French and so fashionable silks and satins, *broderie anglaise*, and skins of minks, and so many boxes of what you call fard, Harry, or perfume, soaps and lotions, brushes of ivory inlaid with silver and finished with pig's bristles, a writing-set in shagreen and a travelling vanity case in powder-blue with enamel stoppers. Oh, I was rich.

I had all I needed. I had my clothes and my cases to keep them in, my scarves and my boots and my linen handkerchiefs with my future initials, J.B., for Josephine Bigelow, and I had my so perfect and subtle materials to cleanse my hair, to service my nails, and to purify my blood. I had everything. I had a twenty-three-year-old future husband running up for his final undergraduate term before graduating at Harvard, and starting his time as an architecture student. Someone whose friends would row for the Varsity crew and whose children, no doubt in time, would be sending in their orders for the design of mansions at Newport. I had all this, Harry. And I had time.

I had nine days left over from Paris, and fitting-rooms, I had an urge to come south and to see what a rest in Venice would do for my nerves. I wanted to pick up a few final items, glass from Murano, maybe, and some peasant embroidery they were talking about in the salons. And, yes, I wanted adventure, too, Harry. I felt the doors about to close on the years of madness, hard and fast if I wasn't careful, and I needed a fling, a throw of the dice on the sand, a bit of a flirting time with nothing to worry about except the disapproving eyes of the old, who were foreigners, and would never see me again, or know who I was.

Boston was coming. Boston with all that its history meant – and you know about it all, you knew it then, Harry – Boston was about to grip its talons and lift me into a frail cell, where I would be cosseted and stifled, and praised and enjoyed, and locked up like a fox.

A pair of lovers. That's what it was. A brace of human figures interlocking. I knew what they called the thing you and I did four days later on the huge cream double bed in my room at the Danieli, the curtains drawn against the sun, and the calls of the gondoliers coming in through the shutters.

They called it soixant-neuf, Harry, for sixty-nine, for the doubled shapes of the two numbers, mouth unto thing, lips unto lips, and it looked exactly like, yes exactly, in the dirty picture you showed me drawn by that old Italian engraver, the shape of the twin parts of the main islands of Venice there in the Baedeker.

I was flushing, sure, when I thought of it later, on the train back out along the causeway, with the rain slanting across the windows, and five inquisitive pairs of Italian eyes in the carriage this time to enquire just why it was that a pretty young girl from America in a short skirt and a veil should be poring over a map of Venice and blushing so furiously on her way home from her holiday. And why, too, she was there at all, alone and unchaperoned, and so obviously attractive to any predatory or footloose man who might be along the corridor.

Of course, it was odd. I'd had to make numerous excuses. My mother, left behind at the Ritz with her smelling-salts and her list of pictures still to be annotated at the Louvre, innocently supposed that I would be meeting my friend Adelaide at the hotel, and be going around the shops and the beaches with her for my nine days of freedom. While my friend Adelaide, innocently supposed that my mother, whom she found stuffy and a thorough bore, would be coming down to Venice, readily accepting my daft suggestion that we postpone our encounter until Genoa, ten days later on.

It worked, Harry. I was alone. Twenty years of pure sex put out on the market, in a slip of a bathing-costume, fine gold as the side of an old sovereign, skin-tight as the kid of an evening glove a size too small. It did things for me, Harry. It did things even when I was on my own in the sun, feeling the hot warmth like a hand on my crutch, like your own hand, Harry, making me squirm, letting me know what my body wanted, and how it liked to be.

So I lay, that first lyrical day, with my eyes closed, under a parasol, and my gun-metal cigarette case open, and a thin lighter gold in the golden sand. My thoughts were fluid, running back along the causeway and returning to the train, remembering how I was all alone in the carriage, the map, how I looked up and out, and saw the glittering stones of the Isle of the Dead, the cemetery, and then the nearer, brighter stones of the city.

From the train to the prow of the vaporetto moving up the canal, past all those palaces and wooden barbers' poles in the stinking water, and watching the stabs of light in the choppy little waves each time it halted. I was helped over the slippery edge of the landing stage by a sinewy arm which gripped me a bit too high under the armpit, brushing the thrusting tip of the nipple under my blouse. I realised then that this was Italy, where a girl is an object of everlasting desire, of eternal admiring lust.

And then the walk with the porter, along the quay, between men selling postcards and some whistling, all of them eyeing my legs, and then over a bridge, and through the Gothic doorway into an echoing hall, all bustling with servants and people coming in and out. There was smiling, and nodding, and 'This way, Signorina,' and into an elevator, all fresh glass and mahogany, with a man all politeness and lust subdued into modes of courtesy. There was a waving of hands, a snapping of fingers, and luggage following slowly, trundling behind, and a pause for a view through a side window of another canal, then keys in a lock, a shutter thrown back. And, oh, Jesus, the flat sudden light, and the sea bursting in, or so it seemed, all bathed in the sun, outside the enormous bay windows, and the man in the duck suit receding, bowing, and leaving me once again alone, surrounded by so much style and glamour and luxury.

I threw myself down on the bed, and stared at the ceiling, decorated with fantastic plaster in roundels and mazes, and then up to the dressing table. I stared at this dazzlingly pretty (so many people have said so), this satisfying and yet weirdly disturbing countenance of mine, before standing abruptly, and taking my clothes off, letting them fall everywhere on the floor, showing me completely naked. You loved it, Harry, the first time I told you all this on the sand – you remember? Your fork rose like a mound in your black trunks with excitement. When I had washed off all the dirt and the mire of the long journey I felt perfect, sweet, sexy, and ready, so very ready, Harry, for whatever might happen that afternoon on the beach.

I took a gondola over, serenaded by the gondolier in the stern as I lay back under the parasol watching the Salute, and the Square of St Mark and the Campanile. And then the line of the lesser palaces all falling back, until I was out on the water, alone with a man too forced by convention to do any more than sing my praises in a language I knew scarcely any word of. And then, far sooner than I might have expected, being there, Harry, at the Lido, at the beach.

I lay in the sun with all this on my mind, in a space a fair distance from anyone else, a lonely-looking girl, either waiting for someone to come back soon and look after her and her casually scattered things, or a young whore, expensive and resting, ready for the next engagement with any bold man sufficiently brave to come up and ask her to dance that night, or come for a swim, or to have a glass of wine.

You did none of those things, Harry. You didn't do anything at all, at first. You were simply there, a black skeleton of a man against the light, staring down, your arms on your hips, when I opened my eyes once. I never knew how long you were there, perhaps a whole lifetime, or only a split second, or a few salacious eyeing minutes, before I woke, from what felt like a long dream of ecstasy, and you spoke.

'Excuse me,' you said. You probably smiled first, even for quite a long time, but I never saw, because you were blocking the sun. You stood above me like a man across the sun, like the human shape Leonardo drew in a circle. Like Apollo, I later thought, in a cradle of fire, or a circus dog that leaps through a hoop of flame, barking with lust. Mixed metaphors, Harry. Very mixed.

You simply lay down alongside me on the sand, so close I could feel your bones, the thrust of your ribs, and I sat up, outraged I suppose, and I saw you as dark as an Indian, a mass of tattoos, like the skilled harpooner Queequeg. Then you rolled on your back and I saw the sun flash there as if it had fallen out of the sky, and taken your shoulder-blades from behind, like a salamander that rapes a pair of lungs. And then you rolled over again, and this time, from being further away, which I suddenly knew I hated, you were far closer. I must have lain back down and closed my eyes again, and your body was over mine like a great sweep of wings, warm as the breast of a dove. I felt your lips like fire, you forced my mouth open, and I was being Frenched by a strange man on a public beach in mid-afternoon with only a thin bathing-costume between us, and I was enjoying it more than I'd ever enjoyed the whole bitter experience, legs open and thing up and all, with any man – including and not excepting my powerful husband Albert – I've ever known.

You knew it, Harry. You felt it through my golden hide, in a quiver of rays, in a bright litter of sudden turns. I was yours. I wanted this. And I wanted far more. And you knew I did. And then we were talking, as if it had never happened, and we were old friends, and we drank sherry cobblers, and gin. We hired another gondola and returned au-pair to the Danieli. Somehow, Harry, you always knew how to arrange these things, and you were in my room, I was across the bed with you above me again. I took from you what I needed, in long bursts, and the sun was drenched in my lap like a pool of honey and milk.

Your throat was still sore. You had had your operation, sharp knives and the red-hot iron, but you healed so quickly in the sun. Caresse was never around on those days we met and strolled in Murano, or out to the little island of Torcello, or back to the Lido, but she was there. On our third day in the sand you told me how you had learned to be jealous, and to hate her lover, the Comte Armand de la Rochefoucauld, a little sandy man of your own age.

You knew what jealousy could do then, Harry, when you'd volunteered to be shot for your rudeness towards the Comte. 'Alas, he laughed,' you said. 'He simply laughed at me, my Fire Princess.' And you laughed yourself, Harry, and rolled over, and took me with my golden bathing costume pulled aside, in full view, so it seemed of an ancient crone with lorgnettes, and in screaming abandon, bottom up and squirming like a stuck pig in the sand. So much lewdness, Harry. So much jealousy leading to this. But there's no need for that any more. You're mine and I'm yours, and we're going to be one, Harry. You and me. Not you and Caresse, because she wouldn't let you realise your dream, your fascination, in a little dim hotel room in New York City, and I would.

Three

Whatever our meeting meant to you then, Harry, whatever it means now, you've had plenty of dreams in the mean time, but there's only one that brings us here. Maybe you wondered whether you would come here to meet me today. Do you feel trapped? I'm no siren, Harry, only an embodiment, a reflection of that one desire no one else could help you consummate.

Think back, Harry, you've always tried to rebel against that safe, secure Boston background. You hate the stifling world we both come from as much as I do. Even as a boy, before the war, you dreamed of escape in the Chinese room, making water bombs. Do you see that Boston boy in the blue sailor-suit, scuffing his shoes off and climbing the polished stairs, pausing, one ear against the wall for the sound of a servant anywhere near, moving up, inching his way along the corridor to the door, turning the handle, and then quick as a kingfisher slipping through and into the airless room? Black. Black and gold. Humming with fierce wasps in summer. Never visited, or not much. Only by you.

Only by you, Harry, the rebel prince in the enemy kingdom, breaking free, loosening the black bow tied at your neck, easing the belt at your waist, not wanting to be, any more or any longer, a little sailor-boy, made in the image of your ancestors, no, not any more. Walking over to the curtained window. Lounging on to the *chaise-longue*. Closing your eyes.

The room was exotic. Unconventional, a strange aberration. A sport. A serious game. The remaining trace of a moment over twenty years ago, when the passing genius of Oscar Wilde, or of Captain Perry, landing there in the bay at Tokyo, with his black ships and his thin cigars, mounting the bridge to speak through a megaphone, had inaugurated a fashion, a taste, a willingness even here in the constricting heart of Boston, to feel the breath of the East. And an artist was imported from New York City, at much expense, and allowed a free hand to line the walls and the ceiling with men in long moustaches, and girls holding fans, and a dragon, twelve feet long, all in gold, and eating his own tail. Eating his own tail in the kind of frustration, you thought, that you were suffering yourself.

There you would sit, Harry, eight years old, hearing the tea-cups far away downstairs in the drawing room, and the echo of your mother's delicate laughter. And you would allow yourself to dream of where the flamingo in his ebony frame was flying to.

Beyond, at least, the brick and mortar of Beacon Street, and the long garden sloping away to the Charles River, and the views across the Public Gardens, and beyond history – beyond the Boston Tea Party, with my own ancestors, Harry, tipping the black grains in the turbulent water, breaking free only to give in, a few years later, to the myth of chains and the bondage of custom in which we both grew up.

So you put your feet on the flowered silk of the couch, rubbing the instruments of the tea ceremony, the Japanese one, with your stockinged, eager toes, and wanting to pick up one of the frail innocent vases toiling with mandarins, and flick it fancifully into the air, and either catch it safely or let it fall. A hostage to fortune. A game with chance. A way, at worst, of passing the time.

But you never went so far. You had brought your own violation, the bright skins of balloons, to be blown up and filled with water from a bucket already waiting in dull magnificence on the landing, ostensibly for fire, a red warning, now to be misappropriated – with what ferocious joy – for the purpose of making water bombs.

You blew them tight, Harry, filling the plump skins from a little jug with a skinny geisha on it. You took it by the handle and dipped, savagely, in the bucket, and then tipped it over the pursed, open neck, slopping lost water over the tea ceremony, and the cushions with views of Fujiyama, and the dusty, celadon-coloured floor that was meant to recall some forgotten temple in the hinterland of Korea.

Then, carelessly still, and with a fine disregard for the metal scorpion, and the toad from Kobe, and a whole slew of netsuke on a lacquer panel, you got the window open, a casement here, thirty feet above the pavement, which was thronged, as you always chose it to be, with people on their way home from work or shopping, and now, uncurling your finger, let your balloons fall, heavy with their burden, to plop, slap and even, delightfully, sometimes burst on the hats and shoulders of the pompous passers-by.

Faces turning up, fists shaking, the screams of maids, girls in long gloves brushing splashes from ruined skirts, an old woman erecting a fragile, white, and somewhat creaky umbrella, imagining rain, a man in pince-nez with a cane and a small suitcase furiously belabouring the door knocker, and Wilson, the imperturbably sedate and soothing butler, appearing, shaking his head in some doubt, holding out a hand as if to feel for more drops, and attempting, often with some success, to unruffle feathers, impress upon those angry faces his own mood, calm things down.

You used to lie back, laughing to burst, Harry, littering the floor with your unused balloons, thumbing your nose, safe above it all, at the stuffy boredom, the stale convention and what you saw, and were surely right to see, as the impossible inflexibility of your enforced environment. You thought you were above it all. And so you were; you were allowed this tiny licence for a while, until one day, by vile

27

mischance, a water bomb had the bad manners to blotch on the hat of the master of the house himself, your dire father, Stephen Van Rensselaer Crosby on his way to the Somerset Club.

'Harry,' says he, pacing the carpeted floor of his quiet study on the first floor, surrounded by leather volumes of law, and a statue or two in perfectly acceptable lewd taste, one showing a Sabine wench in the grasp of a centaur, and one a hermaphrodite in conspicuous bronze. 'Harry, I think, my boy, you have gone too far.'

So you loll back, sullen but unspeaking, and you twist a newspaper in your lap. And you think your own wry thoughts, and you wish he would make his point and allow you to get away to the fuchsia blossom, and the hammock you share with Kitsa, your baby sister. And the hot sun under the gleaming maples, and the endless afternoons outdoors which can still make up for the hothouse constriction of living in 1906, and in Boston society, and of being the heir to a long line of Grews and Van Rensselaers and Beals, who seem to reach out their bony fingers at every opportunity to clog your freedom.

'The Chinese room,' your father says. Then pauses, fingering the silver whistle he keeps on a chain around his neck, and blows every time he hears a joke he finds funny, which is rather rarely at home, and unlikely to be today. 'The Chinese room,' he says, attempting, you feel, a deliberately portentous and severe tone of voice to intensify your boredom and gloom, 'is from this day forward out of bounds. I shall keep it locked.'

This, you feel, rising, and nodding, and sullenly walking to the study door, leaving your father fingering his whistle, and staring as if contemplating an assault with it on the buttocks of the outraged Sabine wench, is exactly the double precaution the moral standards of Boston seem to require. The injunction not to make use of. And the forceful prevention symbolised by the appropriation of the key.

It was on that very day, Harry, that you had your first

vision of Death. You felt a chill, crossing the marble hall. You were drawn, hands in your pockets, idle and annoyed, not as you might have expected or planned out through the french windows and into the garden, where the sun on the flowers caught your eye – no. You were drawn into the little sewing room in the other direction, where the light was colder, and a tall figure sat at a table, working with a needle and thread at a piece of old brocade.

You felt a coldness, you told me, and a strange power drawing you in. Death was tall and old. Sewing in her little room, she was dressed in rustling black. A mutch on her head. The face turned away. The fingers out of sight in a pair of black lace gloves. Working. Working along the grey surface of the stiff material.

'Grandmother?' you said, willing her not to turn. Knowing that if she did, she would show another face. The face inside the face of your grandmother, the face of Death. The face you were suddenly drawn to with a fascination you couldn't control. This was not just the excitement of a child over-exposed to the peculiarly morbid celebration of Boston society funerals, where the event was as relished, formal and expansive, as a wedding or a christening. A ritual and a spectacle. Oh no, Harry, this was a special further fascination of your very own, a secret you kept from everyone, even from me for a while, the secret of your loving adoration of the old lady.

She didn't hear, you said. Or she didn't answer. And so you could walk right up to her, and stand a foot away, watching the hands moving on the grey brocade, hearing the rasp of breath, smelling some strange old person's odour of mould and water, wanting to tiptoe away into the sun, wanting to stay and reach out and lay your hand on the shoulder of Death.

Then you felt a mist rising, a ruddy cloud over your eyes, and as you brushed your face with your hand the old woman must have turned, and you saw that the face you feared and wanted to see had gone, and that your grandmother, a vigorous living woman of seventy-five, was gazing at you in concern, as if you were ill.

'I'm fine,' you said. And then you were walking away, across the hall again, and out through the drawing room and into the garden, flooded with light and sun, turning up your face to feel the heat of it strong on your eyes, closing them, seeming to dream, and then walking into the real garden, strolling under the apple trees and the blossoming lilac over to where your sister was in the hammock, shading her face.

'Kitsa,' you said, 'I can't throw water bombs any more. The Chinese room's been put out of bounds.'

Then you lounged away, across the lawn, reaching up to knock down a handful of apple blossom, feeling the pale, pinkish petals rain on your face, the light blood of the sun, the penance of spring-time, as you strolled through the orchard and under the fading cherry laurel to the edge of the drifting water – Boston water, social water, the avenue for the transport of proper vessels bearing women with parasols to the park, men in their overalls with barrels of things to eat, the intercourse of the day, the transference of the years.

Meanwhile, perhaps, your father paced in the library, wondering over a glass of Russian tea and a biscuit if he had been too harsh, laying his glass aside and rising from a leather chair, pacing arms clasped across his chest, as in a portrait he had seen once of his great hero, Napoleon. He was doubtful still, that eternal man of conscience, very eager not to be too harsh, or to vacillate, or to seem other than reasonable and a just ruler of his house in Beacon Street, his home.

It may have been so. The window open to let in the smell of flowers, the sound of Kitsa, shouting to you, Harry, and your own voice replying, farther off, too far perhaps in its curious echo to please your father, too subtle and wavering in the distance from the bank of the Charles River to seem any other thing that a voice from another country, the land of youth and inexperience your father felt so oddly excluded from.

Relax, Harry, for a little while, for a few more minutes

30

now, and keep on thinking – about your father, about your childhood in Boston, about whatever else you feel rising out of the strange bucket of the past, ready to burst like a water bomb and shower your neatly kept opinions with new freshness. New ideas. Stay back there, Harry, in your own history. Tell me more.

Four

Almost everyone has an uncle, Harry. Yours is waiting for you now in the warm drawing room of his house on Madison Avenue, tapping his lean hands on the top of the sandalwood escritoire in irritation, knowing that this is another of Harry's foibles. You thought he was marvellous once, you thought his money could change the world. And it did, Harry, it did. He financed the war, built a pyramid in his office, wants to buy the world, wants his tea, wants you to admire him still. But when you met cousin Walter, who knew the value of money and its place in the hierarchy of truth, you found another, brighter reflection of something you needed to act on – like me, Harry, a spur. Cousin Walter the writer in Paris encouraged you to be something you'd only dreamed of – a writer in Paris.

Will you go down in that battered, crowding elevator, or take the stairs at a run, and be out in the chill twilight, sniffing the stale steaks in the passageways as you go with your T.S. Eliot always in there in back of your nose, in all your senses, Harry? The special replacement set of percep- tions you bought and had fitted inside your head the very first time you went out and borrowed 'The Waste Land' from a library, or stood in a dusty second-hand shop and laid down your handful of pure gold for a first edition of Pound, or Carl Sandburg even, the petty American Rimbauds of your dream, Harry, the ones who you felt so strongly had to make it. Do you want to hit that evening street in your two-tone shoes with the sunburst on them, hail a cab, ride a few yards on the running-board, like a bootleg hoodlum, Harry, double-breasted suit and all, speaking out of the side of your mouth like Legs Diamond to the driver, 'Take me to Seventy-fourth, Madison, step on the gas, buddy.' It seems those days are over, the play-acting, being a toy gangster.

You have to be late now, Harry. You have to let your Uncle Jack sit there with your wife and your poor mother wondering why you just haven't somehow been able to get to a telephone and send through a message to say you'll be coming soon, and not to wait for tea. There's no choice, Harry.

When I was eight years old we used to go up to Nantucket for the summer, cruising across that still icy water in a low cutter, seeing the spear shape of the island loom and dwell, and then the landing – me first, leaping over the gunwale, skirts up, laughing and running along the flattened sands to the tarred wooden summerhouse on the beach. Mine was there. My uncle, I mean.

He would stand there, smoking a thick-stemmed pipe on the porch, wearing an old blue jersey and rubber boots, taking the pipe out to knock the dottle away and stuff the stem in his trouser pocket, reaching his arms out, free, then, to welcome his eager niece, with her long hair, and her blouse wet with sea-spray, and her wide skirt shaking in the wind as she ran to meet him. Up the steps I'd go, panting already crying out, 'Hello, Uncle John,' and then I'd lunge into the sea-smelling, crab encrusted and tar-tasting environ-ment of his great sweater, making him gasp with affected sudden pain and say, 'Here Josie, take your time, girl, be careful now.'

Then he would bend his unshaven chin and kiss my hair, smelling of smoke more, and of old worn tobacco, and things eaten to keep him going, as if on long voyages, pemmican, maybe, dry apples, juice of some foreign preserved fruit, or the hot quick stink of bourbon, laced with ginger, and under all the scent, the beautiful, sour, male, already familiar scent of a toughened skin. I loved the way he would smell, Harry. He was a man. The first man.

I never knew, of course. Not then. He was my sailor uncle, who used to voyage before the mast in the old whaling ships, and had gone seven times around the world, hauling tackle, seeing the harpoons drive clean into the grey blubber of massive creatures too strange for my own small mind to comprehend except as black dragons, white-fire-spouting wonders of the forgotten oceans under the globe. I felt their power, the lilt and swing of the waves and the whales, the smash of the flukes against the hull, the grind of the stale breakers, the lash of rope and the grit of wheels, the voices of hard men hurling themselves against the bulk of failure – all these were present, though still malevolent and heroic, in the smell and the grip of my uncle's arms.

So he would hug me, seeing the others walking slower with cases and bundles of food along the shore, and his wife would appear from the room behind the mosquito net on the door, and his arm would relinquish what he loved most, I knew, my own sweet skinny waist, and would reach for his wife, and the two of them would be one couple again, welcoming everyone, not just the forerunner, the adolescent mistress, the over-eager, excitable Josephine.

Indoors. Oh, I could go on, Harry. It floods back. The barrels of sherry and fine madeira ranged on the shelves above the stove, like the great ratable barrels in an old whaling inn, which is what his house had once been, the benches cut with the names of the past harpooners, the shadows concealing moth-eaten curtains and rare bottles with carved ships in their blue interiors, ivory drawn from the tusks of narwhals finely engraved with the figures of early nineteenth-century captains, telescopes to their eyes and high sailing vessels behind their loose arms.

Queequeg. Remember? That's what I called you there in the sand at the Lido, the first time you lay down beside me, dark as the skin of an Indian, scored with blue incised lines like the ones on the old harpooner in *Moby Dick*. I knew the book like the back of my hand, Harry, for me it was the history of my own uncle, the last of my family line to go to sea in the ships, to carry the fire for adventure in his belly, like a strange burning, a need for something only the sun and the wind could satisfy. And the whales. The grey speeding torpedoes under the bow, steely as the knives they cut them up with, smooth as the rubber coats they wore, cold as the sea they lived and had to die in.

Queequeg. You looked more like him than any man I had ever seen, even my own uncle, Harry, with the hair under his arms and over his chest like a forest of unbroken timber. No, you were truly the Indian sailor, slender and supple, agile as a cormorant, strong as an osprey, dark as the very sun the Mohicans absorbed in their vitals from years of chasing the buffalo in the dawn. So I took you, Harry, caressing the tattoos, and remembering the curling hair of my uncle which I never dared to reach out and touch when I saw him soaping his back at a twin tub in the tallow-candled kitchen. He was surprised, and a little embarrassed, to see my fascination with the blue snake weaving from trouser top to the hole in his chest.

I had you, Harry, and grasped the history of my ancestors, the long run of black Rotches who sailed before the mast, and were tough and cruel, and grew rich bringing home the oil of whales, and founded their own shops, and their banking-houses, and put on velvet suits, and scented their palms, and took fine hats and high women, and lost, slowly, all that had made them strong, and so came down, through a line of top-hats, and a series of tottering mansions in Boston, to my own time, and my thrown skirts, and my laughing face, admiring their last anachronism, my Uncle John.

I had you, yes. And I dug my nails in, and I came, Harry. Came back to the old ways, and the muscled arms, and the couplings once a year after months of isolation, the dark nights enlivened only by candles and memories, and the sperm stored like the blubber of the whales themselves in a vast hold ready to pour for ever in the fatty groins and the waiting faces of women, wives and bought mistresses, daughters even, whatever the island offered to the stocked, frustrated, anxious arms and pungent members, rocky like fir masts in their heavy trousers, of the huge returning men. Came back, Harry. Came, it seemed, through you, to the whole inheritance of that lost empire, the strange impeccable mastery of the sea, encased in tattoos, in a dark impassable skin. Uncle Harry, Uncle John.

What of Uncle Jack? The sun had blazed for a while for you from his face, when you knew the power his money had to make the dollar flow over drenched Atlantic beaches and reach even to Paris. He seemed like the greatest American alive to you then, Harry. The personification of the great sum of free enterprise.

He found you a job, a job in a bank, a job you held for a little over a year and a half, Harry, such industry. But his power waned. You gave him Indian crabs, paying him off for so many fine meals in that long room in New York, the candles burning the way they do tonight still where he eats alone, I guess, wondering why you never came for tea, and whether his influence has all been to some profit in your life, and whether, after all, the bank was really a place you could ever have made good. His power waned, Harry. And Cousin Walter replaced him.

Cousin Walter. A man of your father's generation. Quite old enough to have been your uncle, and a great cousin anyway. Son of a General Van Rensselaer from Albany, and with hard-riding bones of a military ancestry in every fibre of his tall angular body, ram-rod accurate as his dry mind, his muscular smart opinions, his penned-in emotions, his grace to women, his riding-whip of a way of taking the vulgar down a peg or two.

You met him in 1923, adoring his Degas, the girl dancing you never lost your love for. And his elegance, and his knowledge of French poetry, of French society, and his friendship with Proust and Henry James, and his auto-graphed library, and his access to dukes and princes, his good manners, his taking no shit from anyone. He was what you wanted to be - an aristocrat and a rebel at one and the same time. Or so you thought, Harry.

He died though. The way they all die, the old we admire. The way my Uncle John died, one day as he sat in a rocking chair on the wooden verandah, and toyed with his glass of Jim Beam, and saw the rain come in like the fluke of a killer whale, smite him across the face – and it wasn't rain, it wasn't a killer whale, it was Death itself, in the shape of the grey he had always lived with and feared, and he half rose to his feet, and dropped his glass, and choked, and pitched like a log down those steps to the sand, and turned over once, and was dead the minute his wife came down, a kestrel diving on to a mouse, and reached for his heart.

So your Cousin Walter died, Harry, clutching the hand of Edith Wharton for days on end, saying nothing, only gazing and waiting. Later, they told you – and Cousin Walter was gone.

There you stood when he was cremated, Harry, your dark suit for once exactly in tune, drinking brandy beside the burning coffin, thinking of what the undertaker's men might be joking about in the lower room, and waiting for the heart's (alleged) ashes to be handed over in a little urn. There you stood, Harry, at the crossroads of the sun, feeling the heat in your own vitals almost, and knowing your best auditor and guide to the underworld had already gone on ahead.

Let my ashes, he had said, with characteristic casualness, be tossed out anywhere. So you took them down, Harry, to Edith Wharton's house, and arriving there holding the little cherished urn in your hands, were confronted by two officers of the French police, announcing politely, it seems, but firmly, that ashes were not in fact allowed to be thrown idly around on French soil. Thus, you must, and at once, remove the offending material, and swear in future not to make any attempt to transgress French law on this urgent matter . . . etc.

So there was a quarrel. No, Harry. I know. Not exactly that. A misunderstanding, maybe. About his books. Which – except for such as Edith Wharton may choose to select, and so on – I bequeath to my nephew Mr Harry Crosby, to do with whatsoever he may decide. Thus giving his never wedded and nevertheless no doubt much loved and admired lady friend of many years the option, if she should choose to exercise it, of removing the whole goddamn lot.

She never did. She took only seventy-three. The remainder, Harry, arrived in a series of vans. The first editions of Rimbaud and Baudelaire piled up on top of the eighteenth-century pornography, in tooled leather bindings, the incunabula, the old maps, the rare translated Armenian poets, the disquisitions on the cooking of snails, the treatises on the curing of pork, the works on Japanese lacquer, and the footnotes on Singhalese pottery. Books books books.

You began to feel glutted, to sense – as the great mountain grew higher and higher, a dust wonder, a paper tiger of possibilities, a huge unread momentum of urges and drives and insinuations, a dead weight of culture and leverage, a stimulus and a drag, a serious opening, and a ball and chain on the progress of any writing, or even thought, of your own – that the legacy, far from being an inspiration and a rare delight, was in fact a burden, a responsibility, and a challenge which must be met, and as quickly as possible, by a splendid principle of reduction.

Eight thousand volumes confronted your slow attack. Two thousand more of your own climbed up to help them. You contemplated a drowning. Then took things in hand. You reduced them to nine thousand, then to eight, then to seven. Your plan was to get them down to a single thousand. To a hundred of the very best. To a final dream of dreams: one. The ineffable, perfect, no doubt unreadable, single essential book.

Pressing unwanted memoirs on friends, offering gifts of

diplomatic memorabilia, or insights on gardening, or annotations of minor Tuscan historians, or even sometimes the indices or the commentary volumes of large already dismissed sets, you ended up adding to the paper acquisitions of all your acquaintances, plumping forth their secret libraries with whatever they least wanted.

So that finally you took to the streets, Harry, passing the odd volume to a complete, and no doubt in some cases even illiterate, stranger, leaving the poor man or girl clutching in puzzlement at the rounded binding, the gold spine, and passing on to some stall on the banks of the river, there to slide an immensely expensive prize, unnoticed, and marked in your own hand at an exorbitantly low figure, in between the unappetising mouldy volumes of the cheapest shelves.

Thus did the great man of letters, your hero, Cousin Walter, dissipate, if not as ashes and up in smoke, into a trickle of books dripping away here and there into the vile conduit of everyday reading matter, largely unwanted, and soon forgotten, in your own view, suitably purged of all power to harden or spoil. Poor Cousin Walter. He wasted his only legacy.

Pamela, Harry. Our own wasted legacy. I feel her turning. I swear I do. Her little alabaster skull curling round like a shrimp's head into her tail, pushing, twisting, anxious to take whatever momentary opportunity there might still be to let me know, to remind me of her existence there, to say 'Look, I'm alive, Mummy, I want you to know that, I want to come out, I'm ready, Mummy, I need to be born. Pamela, Daddy. Pamela, Mummy. Give me a chance. Hang on until I can break loose. Give me the life I've earned. I want it now, I want it, Mummy.'

You could stroke her, Harry, where the white skin mounds a little, just a very little so far. You could have waited and seen it rise like a great hill, a white inevitable mountain, bursting with fruitfulness, like a tree of wounds ready to break and purge the pain with its blood of renewal, its girl-child, its wonderful stone at the heart of the body underneath, my womb, Harry. You could have waited. You could have sworn to untie the wretched knot you threw around someone else's neck – I mean Caresse, Harry, your petty stranglehold of nine years of impossible marriage.

You could have slit the rope, Harry. Let the old ship sail free in the brine of tears. Walk away on the dock. Smell the tar and the ozone. Take me by the hand. Smile. Kiss me, Harry. And say, 'Let's try again. It won't be easy, Josephine. It won't be easy at all. But let's try. Only try. Will you marry me, please? Will you give me the child in your clean body to be my own rightful heir, my first begotten one, my true-love-child? Will you share the heat of the sun with me? Burn in the same fire, but for ever? And hold the shared one in our arms, turn by turn? The original triangle. The trio of mutual care, the family group, the core of the holy trinity. Man, wife and child.' You could have done it, Harry, couldn't you?

Five

Whenever your mind goes blank, Harry, it fills with girls. You're a changed man now, though, not reformed, just changed. There'll be no more girls for you now, no more walks to the harbour and times on the beach. When I was a child we used to go along the cliffs of Normandy. Driving, maybe. Or walking, arm in arm with a friend, or a lover, seeing the surf cream on the long beach far below in the wake of the lighthouse, the fishing smacks riding at anchor under the harbour wall, the smoke of a trawler, out at sea, slowly moving with pig iron and tin trays down the channel. Nearer, as you come from the high dunes, picking your foothold through marram grass and the shining, treacherous faces of basalt, yes, much nearer now, you see the old men selling crabs.

I was offered one, Harry, a huge fish-smelling thing with claws, shoved in my face before I knew the value of them, and I cowered back, uneasy there in my pigtails, and the old man smiled at my ignorance, he gave me a gold ring, a little cheap imitation thing that glittered, and pleased my seven-year-old eyes much more than the fruits of the ocean. You know how children are. Little girls. Easily pleased. Aware of themselves and their own strange nature. Sensing trouble in every awkward shape with a strong odour.

We went there often, to the same stone cottage half-way

up the hill, with the Buddleia – lilas de Venise they called it there – in full blossom across the waste land of the garden. I used to run in and out of the low branches wondering where the butterflies lived. There were so many in early September. Tortoiseshells. Like the patterns along my comb. Red admirals. Like the bows they put in my hair.

I spent my summers the way so many American misses did, so many European misses for that matter, dressed in white muslin, with long stockings and flat strong shoes neatly brushed in the morning and thick with mud when the sun was dropping behind the lighthouse at the end of the day of playing. I drank my lemonade and combed my long hair. spoke politely to my parents and the governess, ruffled the dog's hair at his neck, and then bided my time and ran for the dark woods and the gypsy camp, and the men boiling tea in a saucepan, and the boys with eyes like blueberries whittling sticks and swapping rude words about us in French.

Us, for sure. Madeleine and Harriet, Lucy Sprott and Adelaide from the farm, Diana who loved horses, and Lady Jane with the brace on her teeth. We made a fine gang. The tomboys. The girls who took risks, who liked an adventure. I was their leader, Harry. The only one who ever climbed the hollow chestnut and stood in the rotten branch above the main road, waving my legs when a woman wearing a straw hat went by in a limousine. The only one who went up and ran a race around the water meadow against a boy wearing a ring in his ear and a scarf at his waist, and, yes, I was the winner.

France was the same all the way from Calais to Cherbourg after the war. A playground for the middle classes. My piece was Diélette, yours was Étretat. A hundred miles of sand between them. And the same boarded wooden houses, the same women with parasols, the same bicycles and the same berets and the shrewd peasant faces under them. Long rolls cut along the middle and filled with fresh ham or Camembert, baskets of wine and pâté, one-piece bathing suits and trousers rolled up over the ankles. Fathers with pipes and walrus moustaches and mothers rocking prams sheltered under canopies of Brussels lace against the sun.

Somewhere along that shore Proust had gone out year after year as a child in his knickerbockers, gathering into his bullet head whatever would rise later and form the inner crust of his novel, the particular spice and nutshell feel of the seaside, the forgotten ozone and brine world of a French childhood, a pre-war idyll of serving-women in starched uniforms and men expecting their Paris equivalents to chastise them with whips.

Those were the days brushed aside for ever by the war. The whine of the shells and the rattle of ambulances removed those airy drawing rooms and those cloistered bathing-machines. Cabourg was the closed centre. It closed for ever. And the twin wings, the high shore away towards Britanny, and the low shore away towards Belgium, these were its heirs. Clustered with the paraphernalia of the transatlantic intrusion, the carbolic soap and the steam-heating equipment, the cocktail shakers and the steering wheels. Every possible adult means of being comfortable, and enjoying the sea freedom, the sense of being let loose in a massive toy shop, the so endlessly cheap and available shores of France.

But for children things were what they always had been. The opportunity to run wild in the open air, to make unsuitable friends, to be out of sight and mind for a while, away from parents and guardians, to cut legs and get too hot, to spend hours under a lime tree discussing lacrosse or the shape of a ladybird's wings. And for girls – for girl children – the chance, too rare to be missed, of being eyed by improper men, of understanding the unique thrill of knowing oneself wanted, for the much pondered upon and forbidden and indeed little understood purpose, that is, of fornication.

I never had it, then. Never even came near. Except in the long nights beside the open window, hearing the hiss of rain, like a serpent forking a thin tongue at the curtains, and lying so close to a dream the edge grew blurry and unreal, and finding there a tall stranger on a roan stallion, flicking his crop at its withers, and speaking low exciting words in that sort of stage southern accent they always used in the pulp magazine stories I stole from my mother's workbox in the sewing room, and fingered through, and sometimes mouthed aloud, and wanted to be part of, and really, in my childish way, adored.

I might have met you then, Harry. In 1920, when I was twelve. A skinny dark thing in a print dress with a way of drooping my eyes and a quick, sly laugh and a head as empty of any ideas as a Hallowe'en pumpkin. Yes, and with tiny rising breasts as grey as goat's milk – I swear they were – with dark aureoles at the nipples. I used to wash them in olive oil and wonder when they would grow.

That was my last year in Diélette, the year I was old enough for a pony, and left early to learn to ride. I walked on the north shore collecting razor shells, bursting the bladder-wrack with my polished leather toes, and imagining meeting someone as elegant as Rudolph Valentino exercising his borzoi under the cliff. I went home to my frisky pinto, and my tight jodhpurs, and my jars of fragrant saddle soap, and I guess I never thought any more about French beaches and French boys and French kisses and French letters until I was nearly twenty.

It might have been me, Harry. It might have been me you met on the rocks with my shoes off washing sand out of my toes. It might have been me. But you weren't ready for anything quite so out of the Boston mould in 1920. Those were your whores' days, in your cups. Your days of dividing nice girls from tarts. Kissers from chippies. Children with little giggling mouths and moist underarms from dry twenty-five-year-olds with braced thighs and their eyes on the landing stage called marriage.

I was off limits, Harry. Off them to you. But five years on, in Étretat . . . The year, 1925. The month, June. The weather, burning hot. Observe Mr Harry Crosby, banker, of Paris, Boston and New York City, who is reading Chaucer's *Legend of Good Women* and is basking, wearing only a pair of

44

sharply tailored swimming shorts on the flat roof of his sugar-lump of a holiday house. And is drinking – don't forget the detail – a long glass of champagne frequently replenished from a bottle of Krug at his side on the floor.

Enter. Yes, that will happen soon. Enter, dressed in her school uniform still – blue blazer, grey stockings, blue skirt, regulation blue bloomers, grey tie, white shirt etc. – a fourteen-year-old young person of French extraction whom you call 'Nubile' in your diaries. School uniform, although it is now the holidays, and the time is six-thirty, because you, Harry, have invited her so to do. 'I like your uniform. Nice colours.' Yeah. I can see her blush. How do I know, Harry? It was all there for me to see in black and white in your diaries.

What you really saw on that beach as you strolled up from below was the skin of her skinny thighs and her long arms working between the bare toes of her right foot on a rock. Her skirt folded up on her knee, her face puckered, absorbed. As if in sex. As if in lust. I can guess. I know what you like. So you took the jump.

You were all alone on the sandy shore with your so opportunely encountered young female companion cleaning her toes. Caresse was in Paris. You had hired the little sugar-lump with its curtains and its view of sheep from the hill for a period of three months. So you were alone. By night as by day. And lonely. Thus the invitation. Just for a lark. To come over as if from school. 'Much more fun that way, don't you agree – for a glass of champagne? You've never had any before? Well, now, there's a treat. You'll adore the stuff. All bubbles and ice cold and exactly, I'd say, like lemonade. Without the lemon. Much less acid, really. And then, of course, there's a kick. Sort of sting in the tail. You'll love the stuff. If you don't I'll go out then and there and buy you some real lemonade. I promise. Sure. On my honour.'

So up she comes. Her hair in a long pony tail. Her skinny legs in their polished school shoes. A dab of scent – her mother's awful cheap scent, which you, Harry, will very soon talk her out of trying again – in the naughty places no one can ever see. She squats, cross-legged. She takes a sip. She chokes and spews froth. You laugh. She blushes. You reach over and put a friendly arm round her shoulder. 'I'm sure sorry, I didn't mean to laugh. Are we friends? Promise me now. Are we still friends?'

That night you slept on the roof, dragging the mattress upstairs to be in the cool. Alone the first night, Harry, watching her walk home across the cliff, pausing to wave, shaking her child's hair, already meaning to see you again tomorrow even though she said at first she couldn't. So reel on four days. Dance on the beach. Walk hand in hand on the dark sand. Look at the stars. Talk of Rimbaud. And then.

I know, Harry. It doesn't matter. It never happened, you'll say. And if it ever did, it would never have changed the essential feeling. You say, Harry. Sure in your heart or your head that the feeling rules, that the sheer physical enactment never affects what shrills like a bell at the core of the moment, the heart-stopping, head-breaking, earth-opening sense of being, yes, in love – in love with death.

Six

Another beach and another child – you, Harry. 'It used to sing,' you told me. The moment your bare feet scuffed through the white sand of the Singing Beach you could hear a sort of hiss and then a whine, a high, queer note, like the end of a phonograph record, after a piece of good jazz, before the needle finally grinds in the same groove on and on to its own perdition.

'No, it wasn't singing, really, it was more a sound lament of the sirens, I guess, the old world sad for the twentieth century that was going to slaughter its own children. It made a grim sound underfoot, or underheel, rather, but, yes, it got me excited the way flutes do. I used to go in,' you told me, 'whether the black flag for banning all swimming was up or not, and I liked it best when the blue flag for the water being cold was up, and best of all when the black flag was up and the blue was there, too, and I knew it was dangerous and it was icy, like drinking tears.'

Oh yes, Harry, you liked – you still like – that sort of slushy image, it keeps coming, whatever you do, sliming through your best poems, under the guard of your will, mussing up your style, however hard you try to be classical, to be perfect, to be original. But you're not going to make it, Harry. The bad stuff has got you choked, you don't have the time to take yourself to the cleaner's, you're going to be known as a bad poet who shot his girlfriend in the moment after the Wall Street Crash in 1929.

Well. You were in then, crawling fast out away from the safe beach and towards the open sea, feeling the undertow, risking it still, enjoying the sense of being right on the brink, near to your chance of death, and yet far enough only, perhaps, to be sure of coming back, out of that ultimate salt immersion, the lethal womb of the grey widow-maker you knew of from reading Kipling, the killer sea, the lady of the white horses.

Dripping. Ice-cold. Flesh all a-quiver with goose-pimples. Your little curled winkle too shrunk up to allow you to piss out the bottled fizz you had swallowed fast in the larder back home before you came out, that made you burp now, and fill the great fog with your own, more foul emanations.

'I stood naked,' you told me, 'a spindly eleven-year-old, with arms all elbows and legs all knees, and I rolled in the white sand to get dry, hearing the foghorn again, closer now, from the harbour at Manchester, like a beast approaching to eat my bones, all by bones, I thought in my fantasy, and I only there with my bare limbs and a handful of sand to throw in its blazing eyes.

'I was all breaded like a haddock in oatmeal, Josephine,' you said (a better image, that one, Harry), 'and then I felt rough and dirty and I went back in and rolled in the cold surf again to get clean. It was either be cold or be unclean. No other choice.

'Later I walked home through the misty sun, touching the red leaves on the maples, knowing the scent of the Fall as a tremor in my nostrils, a prelude or almost a reminiscence of something expected or known many years before, like dying maybe. It made me sad, but it seemed the kind of thing you had to know to be reconciled to. The kind of thing you would have only once perhaps, and would need to be ready for to enjoy to the full, or live up to. And that mattered. More than a good life, or a happy family, mattered. Or even knowing yourself.

'Sometimes if the red flag was up, for warm water, or worst of all the green flag for only medium water, I would slink home through the grass, and go back to bed, and not swim at all. One day I even went back when the blue flag was out, for the cold, but no black for danger. I was that extreme.'

You still are, though, Harry. I told you that in the tight knot of blankets we rolled into, like two kinds of tobacco inside their own leaves – was it too clever that one, too vague an image – the last night of our time in New York last year, watching the green swoop of the searchlight from the roof of the Ritz. The long searching. The night-long beckoning finger. Like the green light that Gatsby saw at the end of Daisy's dock. Yes. But moving, Harry. Moving.

So go back to your school, Harry, remember the day you went in the fog to Saint Mark's, the tears, your mother doubtful, your father playing about with his whistle, yes, and your own thoughtful slim face, looking back and away at the same time.

Go back to school. Leaf through, in your mind, as you pour yourself the last, or very nearly the last, of the Cutty Sark, those schoolboy days, as you leaf through those shelves of poetry you inherited as part of your enormous armada of books from Walter Berry. Fog, yes. You used to read through the *Encyclopaedia Britannica* from A to Z, systematically. F. Yes. For fog.

The little fog of Sandburg. It sits looking, over the harbour and city, on silent haunches. And then moves on. The great fog of Eliot. Seeing that it was a soft October night. Curled once about the house, and fell asleep. Those two cats. Those two agile, so elegant, so intelligent cats.

'I used to sit up there,' you told me, 'with the blankets drawn over my knees, and look out across the sea, watching the darkness roll in to replace the fog, one even flood of oblivion to remove another, like whisky after women. And I felt my head nodding, Josephine. And then I was fast asleep. An eleven-year-old boy on the sleeping-porch of an old

49

house called The Apple Trees, at Manchester on Sea, in 1909.'

And the fog rolled into the darkness, and they were one. 'As you and I are one,' you told me. Remember, Harry. As you and I. Were one. And will be one.

Seven

Lie on the floor, Harry. Lie and remember. Smell the boot polish and the unwashed linen of school. Smell the aftershave of the geography master, the one who knew how to make the sheets in the freezing north dormitory twist and walk downstairs and engulf you in grave mould. Who could send a shiver right through you turning the wicks in the lamps down, pausing, letting the wind add its own broken litany to the awful tale he was unfolding, and then plunging, screaming or laughing, breaking up his lines to weep, until everyone, yourself included, Harry, would damn near jump right out of your pretty skins.

Those were the evenings you most enjoyed. Hugging your knees, closing your eyes and hearing a voice, talking, telling a story, weaving a spell and frightening you all. And freeing your mind and imagination. Stink of dubbin. Plates of french fries. The rattle of keys in a locker, skeletons in a cupboard. And out of these, like a dark taste of blood on your tongue, Harry, the complicated rustle of lethal machinery, the operatic, eerie mannerisms of poltergeists in the attic, the dragging of a long history of ancestral terror locked in a dripping cellar.

This was the stuff. This was the place where Death could take her boots off, her creaking corsets even, her waxed, slippery gaiters, the paraphernalia of being a woman whom nobody wants in her clothes, only at night, and in bed, someone else's for preference, or on a floor, with a mob of reassuring boys, and a gasp of lust or fear when you put your hand on her bony knee.

So reach up, Harry. You've got her now. Touch the skin of my stocking. There. Just where it rucks behind the bulge of my calf. You can have her all to yourself now. As a pretty girl. As a sweet young thing in a shift and a garter belt. With a certain stiffness, maybe, about her middle, soon to get worse. But still. Your own girl. Your mistress. Your little Josephine.

You dear bastard. You big shot. You lucky stupid idiot. You'd better get up now. No, don't go out through the door. You could, I know. There's the time for that. You've realised. I know. I can see it in your eyes. I had you fooled for a while, Harry. But not for ever. Oh no. Not Harry Crosby. Sure, you can go whenever you want to go, do what you like. You could smooth the skin round your mouth and go right now, Harry, provided you understand that you have to come back. Yes, back. That's all that matters. The coming back. You could run a comb through your hair, and adjust the black gardenia I see you still have in your buttonhole, and take the stairs at a run, and hail a cab, and go over, after all, for a later tea, or to catch them, yes, Hart and your mother and your so adorable big-breasted ageing Caresse, Harry, in the foyer of the theatre. Yes. But I wouldn't, Harry. Not just yet.

Stick around. Think about school some more first. I calculate you could still take a walk through Central Park and buy a hot dog and be back before I get too bad. Do I smell? Buy some scent, Harry. Sprinkle a lot of disinfectant around. Lay down a roll or two of fly-paper. This is the start of the shambles.

But take your time. Remember those other evenings you liked, the serious graduates in their medalled uniforms, answering questions about the war in France, thumbs in their belts, eyes shaded against the far dazzle of the truth, against the real story of what was going on in the mud, unsuitable, yes, in the mind of the Rev. William Greenough Thayer for retailing to innocent children like yourselves on a warm spring afternoon or an icy winter's night in the respectable library at St. Mark's School.

Heroes. Men of Death. Creatures from another, larger world, where the testicles of honour were seized and squeezed by some tighter force than the North Atlantic gales that stopped you passing water some mornings in the outdoor lavatories. Real people, in your view. Survivors. Escapees from the dusty prison of Boston. Europeans.

Well, Harry. The images. The silken abstractions from what they told, the slithering rolled films, chattering out of the projectors laid on raised books on the table top, miming the mutter of the Lewis guns, conveying some images of the true ruin, the ambulances with their wheels off, the wounded with stained bandages on their ears, the grounded rifles. And far above, the aeroplanes, the tiny withering moths, fascinating to your friend Tote Fearing, who would have given his left little finger to be allowed to go as an aviator, to die in the Lafayette Escadrillle, but who was made to do a deal by his parents instead, and went as a driver, and came out alive, as you were to do.

Death, Harry. Death in the mind as 'a belle dame sans mercy,' as the hired man, as nothingness, as the scrape of bones in a crypt, as the fast car hurtling over a cliff in a film, as the moles lying stiff on the lawn all spring, and, yes, most of all as these tattered scraps of cloth and strutted wood scaring like black paper out of a bonfire, the crackle of the Somme, the SE 5s, the Camels, the German Fokkers.

Death took you over, Harry, death was your bride, your little mother, your bleak sister. Five years had been shut away like a precious ornament in a box. Five years of keeping your boring diary, and admiring the peppy French maids, and masturbating into a can of paint, and sometimes going home for tea on Sundays, hearing the whine of your father's whistle in the distance, like a steam train with a cowcatcher pestered by Indians on a lonely track of line in the heart of Wisconsin. Well. Five years. From a boy of thirteen who could swim well and run a bit, and was always punctual – and is always surprisingly punctual still, Harry – and who cribbed his math and Latin, and who gained no special honours at games or for academic excellence. From this boy to a good-looking, slightly-built and spectacularly attractive eighteen-year-old who had become available to the lethal, the world of killing.

How did it happen, Harry? How did you lose that intangible innocence, that awareness of being only one of the crowd, a regular guy, a rather quiet and not especially striking supporting lord. What made you lean forward out of the rigging and ask for a turn at playing Hamlet?

Someone, I guess. One of those fluttering girls you were always kissing during the holidays, one of those giggling boys you were often fondling, dirty in your football knickers behind the pavilion. Or being fondled by. Or being kissed by. It has to be someone, Harry. Someone who let you down, or put you down. Someone you wanted, and couldn't have. Maybe an older woman, a bitch with the hots for you, pulling back, sated. Or a boy too young to care to go on, or in. Or Easy, even. Your poor dead dog, who died one summer afternoon in the year the English went to war, and was laid in the earth under a stone at Manchester.

The abandoner. Whatever his name, wherever her home. Someone who pulled out and took off into the sunset, riding or not willing to be ridden, and planting for the first time that furrowed arrow in the soft places of your skin, the poison head, the sense of the best things not being there, after all, for ever and ever. But only on loan. Only for now.

You stepped up the gangplank of the *Espagne*, bound for France with your friend Tote, and seven hundred others, not all volunteers, not all, for that matter, men. And what led you to put your name down for the American Field Ambulance Service, to accept the destiny of a soldier, and the chances of death? I think it was some incident you kept back from me, something that hurt you, not merely the usual patriotic or adventure-seeking motivation that sent your generation to its doom in the mud.

'We were ten days on the crossing,' you told me, 'hearing Cole Porter and his group from Yale singing his wised-up songs at the ship's piano, or a kind of zither rigged up with a keyboard. It was fun, Josephine. There was nothing much to do, just watch the sea, neck with the girls, take part in the lifeboat drill, and dream of medals.

Take a deep breath, Harry. Do better than that. What thoughts used to come into your head in the little sweltering cabin, lying back on your bunk at two in the morning, with Tote and your other fellow passenger snoring, and the ship rocking in a mid–Atlantic swell, bells ringing maybe. What thoughts of the past mixed in your mind with the coming visions of mud and glory, sifting through the jazz, the women's voices filtering out of the corridor, the stale taste of your bad supper under your tongue?

Tell me, Harry. I'm here to listen now. To be your silent mouthpiece. Tell me the true story.

Eight

Put your head on my shoulder, Harry. Cry a little. There. I know what it's all about now. More than I did. More than I did then, alone in the Ritz, with your face on my trembling clitoris, and that strange invisible ghost of a smell black in your nostrils, blotting out what I was, Harry, a living woman. Smelling of scent. Smelling of cypress leaves, and of gin and garlic.

You changed the smell, didn't you, when you remembered the trauma of war in your diary:

> Ten years ago today on the hills of Verdun and the red sun setting back of the hills and the charred skeletons of trees and the River Meuse and the black shells spouting up in columns along the road to Bras and the thunder of the barrage and the wounded and the ride through red explosions and the violent metamorphose from boy into man.

Was the war really so neat? Remember, Harry. Remember 741, the number of your ambulance. The holes torn in the earth. The wheels grinding in mud on the hill to the abri. You told me. Remember. There on the floor of the Ritz, with the green light swinging, out and back over the night city with all its glamorous opportunities and liaisons. And I on my back satisfied, with my skirt up to my waist, all beads and French silk and chiffon, and listening, taking it all in. The sense that this was the thing you most wanted, to make me a privileged acolyte at the ritual celebration of, your first and most memorable death.

Twelve years ago and a bit now. The Ford was turning outside the abri, and the engine stalled, Spud Spaulding standing laughing in the doorway, only a yard away, his jacket open, his own ambulance parked in the rear, both of you waiting to load up and ride back to the hospital, nobody else nearby, the first shell landing forty yards away, nobody bothering, then the second – this is the one, Harry, this is the one they all tell you about, the one with your name in silver carved in the nose, yours and Spud's, a pair of names only for this one, the one that's out to get you.

That's what you told me, Harry. That's what you told me the night we lay on the floor of the Ritz and played blind man's buff with a thimble lost in the folds of my knickers. 'Shells, Josephine. They toil not, neither do they spin.' And then you said, 'I mean, they do spin. They come out of the rifling shit-hot with muzzle velocity of Christ alone knows how many feet per second or miles per hour or blood spirits per infinity, twisting up there into the black sea of the sunlight, falling, falling. Until you wonder how much of the solid sky is sheer shrieking metal, blue with steel, red with flame, and the only thing to do is bury your face in the stink of the mud, and wait for salvation, for death, for a quick release from pain and fear.

'Oh yes, they spin all right. And they toil, too. If you consider what packed, intensive energy it takes to pull a human body apart, and leave a man no muscle there in his jaw to scream with, no legs to run away on, no bloody penis, even, to reconcile his nights to the absence of women with. They have to toil in a sense to get all that head of steam up to be vaporising iron, and landing car wheels like baseballs on the roofs of high churches. Toil, yes.

'But not in the sense the poor superstitious French convent-school or something similar conscripts used to think. Working, I mean. Working the will of God out with a deep and unseen purpose in every sudden, inexplicable, shattering éclat. Deciding the ones to live and the ones to die, and with reasons beyond the mind of man to know, but reasons. The French are very big on reasons, Josephine. They used to go down to the priest or the padre on Sundays and tell their sins and twist their imaginary mental worry beads and do their penance and wait for the next shell to step off to the left and take its cap off and say, Sorry, monsieur, I almost forgot that you were one of the saved, forgive me.

'I never saw it happen. The shells just went on weaving and spinning, the way they always did, and the men were wounded and died, and we carried them out of the dressing stations into the Fords, three at a time, and one of us drove and one of us did his best to make them comfortable, or to comfort them, and the shells neither spun nor wove any fancy pattern at all, they just fell and fell like the rain, heavy on the just and the unjust, and particularly, if you want to know what I think about patterns and choice and the will of God or whoever, Josephine, on the innocent, on the very many who deserved a little better of the world.'

Flump. Kerflump. You were down, by some magical anticipatory instinct, on the floor of the Ford, face down perhaps in the kind of act of adoration before a superior power you do now for the sun, but out of the flush of the blast, at any rate, the blast that ripped white moths of flesh out of Spud Spaulding's chest above the heart and spattered them over the backboard you were leaning against only seconds before, failing to find you, failing to find another vulnerable breast to be mingled in, as you lay, the air ringing with all that had missed you, like the sound of bells for a wedding, the miracle of your deliverance.

Later you drove back through the shell-field, Weeden there in the back with Spud's head in his lap, shot full of morphine as you both sang, calming what shreds of nerves you had left with 'I never raised my boy to be a soldier', and the moment was gone, the miracle over, only the memory of it there for

58

ever in your very cells to be lingered on, and studied, and lusted for again, Harry, I see that now, wanted another time, the proof that you out of all the world's American soldiers are singled out for the special protection of Theodore W. God, Esquire.

Six months in the hospital. Six months for Spud, and he was fine. More or less. Give or take a little. Err on the generous side. The miracle had its side-effects, it seems. Those close enough to your luck to be in the same tent, or the same set, the Hounds as you called yourselves, or the House of Lords as the rest knew you, the privileged few, the élite – well, after all, you boys were going to get through with only the minimum amount of pain, it seemed, no brutal maiming, no mortal wounds et cetera, not for those in the charmed orbit of Harry Crosby, no sir.

Yes. You were good on the shells, Harry. Paid a nickel a day to be out there under them in all weathers, but mostly when it was wet and freezing, with your hands on a slippery wheel, and your glasses on to see the shell-holes, and no lights, except from the flares or the shells themselves, or the phosphorescence of putrefaction, the slow corrupting essences of the dead horses, the dead men in the mud.

There was nothing to keep your own sides from the hell of tearing except the paper-thin edges of those ancient solitary ambulances. They had a tendency to stall, and awful gears, and no windshield to keep out air or blast or bullet. Well. You worked hard, Harry. You were worked hard. The war had you, and you paid the fee.

'Smell,' you told me. 'That was the worst, really. It never let up. The sound was terrible. When the great bombardments used to start it went on and on until you began to feel walled up in the skin of a drum, until you began to become the skin of the drum yourself. And then you felt sick, and then you felt frightened out of your wits, and then you felt nothing was left except to be angry, and anger built up and up until you were strong enough to burst out of the drum, even strong enough to pick up the whole screaming sky of pain that the drum was and burst it across your knee, or the butt of your rifle. And then you charged. If you were an infantry man, that is. You put your bayonet out on the end of the Lee Enfield, and you speared the Boche. That's how they went over the top and into the wire, most of them. The sound helped, in the end. It drove them crazy, with sheer rage.

'The smell was worse. It shocked me, at first, and then I got used to it, and then I forgot. And then, gradually, it slipped its knife in again, and you started to see that the worst of the smell was just that it was always there. Mud everywhere and that foul, shitty, macabre smell, odour of God knows what that just oozed and sweltered and froze over all your senses. You seemed to swallow it out of a beer bottle, chew it for beef, see it splotch on your clean shirt, if you ever had one, crawl out of the soup tureen the day you had leave and went for lunch at the Crillon. Stuart Kaiser said it was cut in lengths and papered over the walls of his lungs. He could never get it off.

'I smell it now,' you said, 'sometimes now, even, when I breathe in the cleanest air on a spring morning. The smell of the front. The smell of the abri. The smell of the Argonne sector. The smell of Verdun. Seventy thousand men killed on a single morning had made their contribution to that smell. One for every foot held on the Front.'

I was only ten. Still at the crush stage with the gym mistress. Reading the newspapers. Probably ready to hand out my white feathers to the men who wouldn't go. I hadn't even been kissed. I blushed when I took my knickers off to wash myself. I was that young. Sex was as far away as death was. As far away as the silver cups on the shelves I never won for doing anything very clever.

Well. We grow up quickly nowadays. We girls. We people, Harry.

Nine

Driving golf-balls into the sea. That seems to sum it up, after the war. The waste and the violence. You had to have something, all of you, ex-fighting-men, adventurers drawn away from the fields of glory with nothing left to live for, blind action, even, something at any rate to exercise your muscles on, swinging away in the morning before dawn, or an hour or two after sun-up, there on the cliffs near Manchester. Near Situate. Anywhere north of Boston.

I do know it was all so romantic, being young, being a man, after the war and the action. Veterans all of you, knowing the ropes, knowing the face of death, sure thing. You all knew what a corpse was like, what a stiff was. But how to give pleasure, or even a sense of being alive, to a fresh young girl in a low party dress, after a tot from your flask, even, why you were slow in that, Harry. You all were.

I had another uncle, you know, an uncle who put his hand where he never ought to have when I was eleven years old, Harry, that very war. My own uncle, Henry Schuyler, another veteran soldier, but with no more confidence of his chance of getting his way with a real girl in camiknickers than you had then, with no more sense than to pull his thing out and show it to someone who hadn't the space in her sailor suit to push it in, and never wanted to, and ran away, crying and crying, but not before he had had his dirty hand on her thigh, and higher, too, Harry, murmuring, 'Kiss me, kiss me, Josephine. Please kiss me. It'll be all right.'

It wasn't though. It wasn't all right at all. Not then on the swing seat in the garden, hearing the bees hum in the lime, right up and up like a long drone rising to reach the clouds. Not then, no, nor later, sobbing alone into a green brocade cushion. Not knowing who to speak to about it, or what to say, or why it had happened, and where for a terrible moment, the old nice gentlemanly Uncle Henry had gone to. Pulling his trousers open, and showing that fat, whippy sausage there.

I didn't want to see. I didn't know what it meant. But I do now, Harry. I can take a lot in my eyes now, in my mouth even, I couldn't face when I was eleven years old. When I thought the only thing about men in love was their bringing boxes of chocolates round, and standing shifting their feet, and maybe blushing, too, and not knowing what to say. When I hadn't even seen the Doberman bitch in the shrubbery, or heard the under-chambermaid when the butler lay on top of her in the larder. No. There has to be innocence, Harry. There has to be time.

I wasn't ready then. I wasn't ready for the whole stampeding, galvanised, unnecessary aggressive sexuality of men. I was just a little girl with her hair in a pony-tail, and a pair of long scarred legs from climbing trees. And a liking for horses, and maybe, yes, I agree just maybe, a pert way of looking up at men from out of the corners of bright eyes – but only for fun, I didn't know what it did to them, God, I swear, Harry, I never knew.

So there you were, the four of you, Weeden, Spaulding, Kaiser and Weeks. Drunk as lords in the Stutz, heading at sixty miles an hour in the dead middle of the cliff road for whatever the night might have waiting for you. Betting or women, more whisky or black Russians, this was the 1920s your car was driving fast into, the amoral decade of the beautiful and and damned, although none of you was old or experienced enough as yet to be able to get what you wanted.

Look at yourselves, Harry. The famous four. The House of Lords. Each with the Croix de Guerre bright as a dull bronze penny in back of your brains. The third-class distinction – not as good as a Medaille Militaire, not even as good as a Légion d'honneur – the essential bottom line for the soldier anxious to show he had had his nervous rocks off in the firing line.

Stuart Kaiser, long-eared as a donkey, smoking cigarettes in his ivory holder. Ted Weeks like a nimble sea captain, stocky and merry. Tote at the wheel – after all, this was his car – like a broad-browed implacable steam-turbine, iron-faced, iron-hearted. And you, Harry, already perhaps in one of your early black double-breasted suits. With your nails painted ebony, and the flask in your thin fingers, crew-cut as you were with the wind ruffling your hair. You were wild, the four of you. Wild. Or wanting to be.

But you weren't all that rebellious, Harry, not so rebellious that you could help wanting your time at Harvard, signing on for English and French, easy options, a bit of Spanish, Fine Art, nothing to trouble your tired wits with, or to take your time up, or your mind off girls and whisky and high old jinks.

Harvard, the brick and ivy school. The place your father had been. The signing-on room for the A.D. Club. And you got in, Harry. They saw to that. The string-pullers. The friends of your father, whoever they were. The old gang. It took a trio of rounds, and a couple of years, but they got you in. A dubious honour, as one might say, to be thought worthy of membership for the future dinners, a time or two a year maybe, but not for the day-to-day unavoidable under-graduate companionship.

So back to the car. Back to the wheels grinding in gravel, the last stop. The sun rising behind the barn, and the engine steaming in front of a classical porch, as you pile out, all of you, drunk and stiff now, giggling maybe, ready to wake up your friend, a Morgan maybe, or a Grew, or a Wiggles-worth. 'Shhh,' says Kaiser, putting a finger up to his lips

'Shhhh,' you say, lifting your flask and taking a last swig.

'Shhhhh,' says Tote, and lays his hand on the rubber bulb of the horn, until Weeks, dear merry little Ted, the sober one for the night – there was always one of the four, wasn't there, Harry, who kept his head, who had nothing to drink, who could drive maybe when the other three were out cold – pushed aside his hand to stop the noise, and you all walked round the side of the house and went in through the french window, sniffing the dawn air, and felt through the house to your friend's room.

The four hands on his shoulder, the comrade-in-arms, or out of them, rubbing sleep from his eyes, grinning, alone in the bed, sliding his hand under the pillow and drawing out – my God, you were all impressed by this, Harry – a black silk stocking.

Those were the days, they were. Or were they? I wonder. The days before you had, any of you, the power you have now, some of you, one of you, anyway, to be handling the merchandise with more skill, getting it in and out of its packaging, Harry. Amateurs then, not yet initiates of the golden mystery, the way to be causing the triangle to moisten, the mound to grow wet, the woman to weep with tears of love. You stupid bastards. You idiots. You young men.

You knew nothing. Only the way to buy a pair of cheap stockings in a dime store, and burn one on the rubbish heap, and stuff another under your pillow to kiss and croon over and pull out when your friends came in drunk. And to show off, and be admired, for having a trophy, drawn from the living flesh, torn like a scalp in the virgin wars. Well. There were many of those. There still are.

So back in the car. Envious now. A little quieter. Dreaming of how you, too, could be sleeping the sleep of the satisfied, with a girl's black skin shed for love in your sheets. Engage the gears, Ted. Run around a while. Cruise up along the north shore and let's see the sun. Shirred eggs later for breakfast at Diamante's. 'Eggs Benedict?' Well, whatever you say, Tote, whatever you say. It's your car, after all, goddammit.

But you make one more stop on the way to your late breakfast down-town near the Stock Market. One more stop. A mile or two above Coffin's Beach, to see your old friend. Another Wigglesworth or a Sturgis or maybe a Monks or a Beal this time around. In his neat slacks and his crisp new-laundered shirt. A hundred yards from the house with the green shutters his father built out of oil or railway stock and furnished with European glass. Outlined against the dullish red orb of the rising sun. Driving his golf-balls into the sea.

One swing, and the first went far out and high like a well-aimed grenade lobbed into a German trench. Another swing, and the second went low and into the shingle, and made a noise like machine-gun fire. I guess like the rest of you he was in the American Field Ambulance Service, and never fired a shot in anger the whole war long. He lay under those everlasting bombardments, hearing the shells whine the way you had yourself, Harry, wondering, too, which one might be there with his name on it. Knowing nothing later would ever matter so much as having come home, with a whole skin, and a bunch of years to live through, and nothing at all he could think of, worth while, to do with them.

So he got up at sunrise every day, and put on his clean civilian clothes, after washing and shaving, the way he could never do at Verdun. And he took his bag of clubs, and a stock of balls, each one monogrammed in red, so that when he had let it ride high and into the sea his gardener could see where it fell, and retrieve it, rowing out in a boat from the beach.

Driving golf-balls into the sea. Nothing more pointless. Nothing more suitable, so it seemed to me, when you told me, Harry. Nothing more likely to seem just right at the end of a night's riotous drinking. Driving around. Meeting folks. Doing nothing. Aimless and amiable. At least with your friends. Your three fellow Hounds.

I want to get up now, Harry. I want to go downstairs and tidy my hair and then come back up and have one more Scotch. Then we can do it. Or maybe go out instead for some dinner or take in a party or something. I don't know. Nothing more pointless. Well, maybe. Nothing more aimless, except to be lying here without moving. Without being able to choose. The way you're going to be yourself, Harry. In time.

Ten

Your wife, Caresse, she was the first to do so many things. She was the first girl scout, for God's sake, meeting the wife of Baden-Powell at Rosemary Hall. She invented that brassière. She must have had lovely breasts in those days, tying a silk handkerchief under their droop before a ball, and going in without a corset. Sure. She was the first, I give her that, who really made you feel what a woman could mean. Caresse, yeah, I guess it suited her then. Better than poor little Polly Peabody.

I see her now in her little sweat-shop in Washington Street, supervising the manufacture of the wire-less affair she later patented and sold to Warner Brothers. I see her calling herself Valerie Munro, avoiding the casting couch as best she could, and still believing she had a future in films. She always wanted to be her own woman, Harry. A business tycoon. Or a film star. A book publisher or a lady with lovers. It didn't matter. She wanted to be somebody, and not just *Mrs* Somebody. You knew that but you didn't know what it had to mean. She had to grow or die.

What's she doing at this minute, Harry? Fitting the crust of éclairs in her mouth over there with your uncle, crossing her thighs over dreams of her lover, the leathery aviator, in Paris. Wondering when the powder will crack, the varicose veins go in her calves, the bird's lines break out and walk from her eyes down to the sides of her lips. After thirty-seven lover-filled, breast-thickening years she isn't the same. She knows she isn't. Well, who would be? It's a hard cool world, Harry, the women come and go, talking of Michelangelo, or whatever else they want to talk about in the steaming drawingrooms, the cold-water flats with their husbands, their lovers, in tattoos, in shirtsleeves, their oblivious rich paramours in their silken tuxedos, their yachts and their manicure artists. They come and they go, then they grow old, and they don't get cared for any more as they used to, and everyone knows they don't, even you, Harry, dreaming however you may of an ever-lasting love affair in the skies or the doldrums.

It was in 1920 that your mother introduced you to poor Mrs Polly Peabody née Phelps Jacob, little thinking how you might scandalise society by running off with a divorcee. Oh, I know she was pretty, once. She was a spoilt rich girl like me, with a drunk husband and nothing left after the bells ringing except a lifetime of cocktail parties and looking back with old school friends over all the years spent learning to skate and ride and go to Mr Dodsworth's Dancing Class in the days when there weren't too many Jews on the rolls. She was a snob, Harry. When Boston disapproved of her divorce and love for you, she cared.

So how was she, Harry, the day you sat on her right at lunch and ignored the girl on your other side, already fascinated, the way we've all seen you, the moment the new girl appears, the fresh inspiration of your perennial death-wish? How was she? Did you know then what it felt like to be thinking, always, in the back of your mind, of an ex-soldier who cared only for booze. Who hated his own children, or at any rate the mess they made, the same way you do, Harry, surely the same way you do. And who loved, sure he just loved, you say she said, to lie in his bedroom night after night with a fireman's helmet on, and an axe beside him, waiting to hear the gong ring above his bed with a major alarm. They say he contemplated slipping a pole down from the room to the garage below to get out to the fires faster when the calls came.

Then they stopped all the private firemen, with a new law, and he had his drinking left, only his booze to help him forget the war, and his need for something to do, something romantic and wonderful to take his mind away from the kids bawling. Yes, he was much like you, Harry, I can see he was. You must have appealed for being the same, really, not for being different. Yes, for being a drinker too and a crazy fool obsessed with fires, only your fires all concentrated in one, the heart of the sun.

I can imagine how Caresse felt, getting her man back from the war, finding him still away inside a bottle of Scotch, his only dreams of a house burning, his worst fears of being left indoors alone with a screaming baby. And then to meet you, Harry. With all the same wildness, and all the same faults, and a face like a white hatchet smiling out of a flame-thrower. And the charm. The charm of a prince.

It was only seventeen days you told me before you became lovers, before you went over the top with Polly – Caresse, over the top, sure. Those were your words. Over the top, the way the infantry soldiers went with their bayonets fixed, and the field officers with the whistles between their teeth like your father. Over the top and across the open ground and into the wire. The tough, bristling wire in her groin that bewitched you.

I still know what it's like, Harry. I haven't forgotten the Lido. The sound of the waves and the sand on my thighs. I haven't forgotten the way you speak when you've had your fill. The way love starts in your heart, or whatever it is, when lust goes out the window. Like all men. Like Albert, anyway. He was just the same. A flood of tears and protestations the moment it seemed the desirable place in the dark valley might never be open again, except, maybe, for the babies coming.

Love. What a strange mismanaged excellence it seems to have been, Harry. For us. For everyone, perhaps. Lying together and then lying together. Wanting the closeness of bodies only, the abrupt fall far over the precipice into the glittering abyss of intense forgetfulness. And then the caring. The greater closeness. The for always factor.

You were always affectionate, Harry. Even after your marriage, and all that romantic afflatus, you never changed. Caresse couldn't stop you. While you lived out your dreams in a world of steamboats and saloons she entertained herself and waited for your return. But not now, Harry. No more returns to your forgiving wife. How many women were there Harry, can you remember?

You mention so many names in your cups, Harry, turning over on the pillow after making love, with a different face in your dreams, another memory, another anticipation, maybe, Constance or Jacqueline, or whoever else there is for a brief second parting her thighs in your thing's eye. Carlotta, yes. More than one time, with her gold hair and her soft eyes and her tightly woven basket of first-class goodies. You were with her in Switzerland, one February, snowshoeing down-hill together in the darkness towards the lights of the small hotel, hearing her life history, like so many more. The perfect listener, Harry. The perfect lover, too, no doubt. The perfect friend, when you took her out to a whorehouse in Paris, and sat with her and eleven daughters of joy, speculating on their qualities and on hers too, no doubt. Carlotta, Boston Joan – and who was 405?

You made a mistake letting me go through the manu-scripts of your diaries, you know. I have a mind like a camera. I photographed the lot in my head. I have them there like a set of prints, the long and the short and the tall, the laid and the flirted with, the desired and the had and the wanted, the rich and the poor, the lewd and the innocent, the ones in their lace pretties and the ones held squatting down and spanked with a slipper. You kept them a good secret, most of them, vague and sexy, distant and almost recognisable. Almost, yes, but never quite.

You were with 405 on the very day you went up to Long

70

Island to confirm your job in the bank in Paris with Uncle Jack. That job was the only way you could do a deal with Polly, who was getting difficult now, the only way you could have her near, living in Paris beside you, but not getting married, no, Harry, she was still trying to draw the line at getting married. That same day, you borrowed the old man's brand new automobile and drove it down the Arlington subway until you smashed on an iron fence, your face off the road and your lips crushed on 405's in the side seat, with her sequinned legs tangled over your lap and a bottle of bubbly open and foaming on to the floor. You were lucky, both of you, not to be thrown through the windscreen and killed.

I know you, Harry. She was still there a month later, with Polly off in Paris, part of a threesome with Lou Norris. Domestic bliss, maybe, or a squalid little closeness not altogether to be reconciled with your grand story about the sun crashing in silence three thousand miles away and your heart bursting with loneliness.

Well, it burst. I grant you. Or so your actions would seem to support. You always did have to have — everything, everyone. So you sent a wire from Paris the moment you docked for your new job, and you blew seventy dollars on a one-way ticket to follow Polly to England, to the land she had escaped to, and you landed out of the sky, in Polly's lap amidst the croquet, or the flannelled English fools at their tennis, the blond hero, the desperate eager one, and it worked. Sure, it worked, Harry, and she fell in love with it, and in two days you were both on another aeroplane, and the Channel was lyrical blue down below, and the ships fluttered their flags just for you, the two of you, Polly and Harry now, not set on their way to be married, no. But for living together, you at the Metropolitan, for address purposes, but in fact, and for fun, and for fornication, with Polly Peabody at the Hotel Regina on the Right Bank. Yes, you can do a lot in a single room, Harry, in a single bed. It makes for closeness. We both know that, don't we?

There were good times, Harry. Booking a taxi all the way to Deauville, and the metre breaking at four hundred francs. Taking a room together in Venice – our own city, Harry, our own damn city, for God's sake – as the Viscount and Viscountess of Myopia, the name of your father's club in Boston. Irony and extravagance. Have I caught the note? And meanwhile the infidelities continued.

Why do you do it, Harry? Why did you do it then? I can see you pinning your little chart up on the wall after she'd gone. The paper divided up into squares, a hundred of them, each one inch long, and the names of all your vices transformed into horses: Nocturne for late nights, Masked Marvel for girls – a give-away that, your taste for disguise and deceiving more than for solid unambiguous flesh, I'd say – and Smokeplumes, I like that one best, your name for cigarettes. They went forward a square when you gave them up, then back a square when you sinned. I doubt if the poor Masked Marvel ever had a chance of coming home in the first eleven, Harry. She must have been several feet behind the field in the very first week.

With Jeanne, for instance. The virgin from the Bank you drove down to Deauville – never miss a chance of repeating a good idea, Harry – and then sat beside and lusted for while she dried her clothes after a thunderstorm in front of the fire at an inn. I can imagine the bottle of wine and raw flame. The girl's naked arm, and then her waist, and then the unbroken shadow between the hips and the lips not touching but not violating. So you say, Harry. So it was, maybe. You like to frustrate yourself some days. But what happened to poor Jeanne later, on the page you didn't enter into your diary?

You couldn't wait, though. You had to have her, your Polly I mean. So you bet a friend a hundred dollars you could be in America before he could, and borrowed the money from the bank, and booked your passage across on the *Aquitania*, steerage. Well, Harry. That was quite a change. Quite an adventure. Down there in the stink of all those common bodies you had a chance to think for a while. You had a chance to eat your full of bully beef and boiled potatoes. It took you three days.

You docked, and Polly, there before you, met you at the barrier. You were married that afternoon. It took you twelve days to write any sort of commentary in your diary, and then what was it? I remember, Harry. I took the photograph in my head with a lot of care 'Read *Les Désenchantées*. *Am I?*' Twelve days. It hardly sounds like the perfect honeymoon.

What time is it, Harry? What time is it now in your head, I mean. Are we going to be married soon, married properly this time, in the only way that really matters, and for ever, and without any possibility of divorce or second thoughts? Are we, Harry? I wonder.

How many days was it before you realised what had happened in the chapel of the Municipal Buildings in New York City? It wasn't the perfect suicide you expected that time, Harry, was it. It wasn't for ever. It was for never, you started to fear. All that energy that had gone into getting things organised for the push, the final orgasm of completion, had expended itself, it seemed, on itself. There was nothing left for a while.

Only her children filling the house with their noise and their mess. Only Billy and Polleen, waiting with their nurse at the Belmont. Only Billy and Polleen, who were ordinary American infants, and not the dream children you had had in mind.

But the children were yours, although they were not yours. They were in your house, they were there when you least wanted them, leaving their sticky draggle of fur animals, and their boxes of broken games, and their half-eaten, half-drunk, unappetising meals, and their unwashed, so it seemed to you, Harry, unwashable dishes. Billy and Polleen, two inevitable adjuncts of your most lascivious or romantic impulses, crying out for attention in the midst of undoing garter-belts, or rushing in imagination through catalogues of foreign tours. Two dirty and squealing obstacles to the sudden journeys. Making their mother drop her golden robes

73

and put on more comfortable, unclinging things, and play on the floor like a fattening, ageing, middle-aged momma, and not be for always a wicked mistress in a black suspender-belt, with her mind on sex and Afghanistan. Demanding. Needing. Intervening. Making you take, for however short a time, Harry, the second place.

Eleven

You called being twenty-five the halfway mark. But maybe you felt it was more the last lap already, being married and working in a Paris bank, feeling the clog in your pores, the fat gathering round your heart, the years taking their toll. So where were you running? What were you running for? To think? To get away? To feel free? Or to work the chains off your ankles?

Running, yes, And canoeing, too. Down the Seine each day from your flat overlooking the water, with its balcony and its view of Notre Dame, its view of the shameless girls swimming, the unchaste Seine girls, as you called them. Bosoms and bottoms bobbing down below in the big swimming race, and you up above with your one true love, in a high window, watching, calling out maybe, and waving but never touching.

Day after day in your smoky office at the bank, shoving the messages aside, taking a day off, a week off, a lifetime off in your mind, as you started to read, with that meticulous dedication we all find so very surprising, Harry, book after serious lengthy book, and the dictionary was the first. So you soon knew what an aardvark was, and, later, a xebec.

Escape, that was the question. Out of the chains of the swivel-chair, and the forthcoming pension, the share options and the seat on the board, out of the manacles of the state of marriage. Into the freedom of literature, the opportunity to say and be what you wanted, yes, that's what you wanted, and then you saw that literature was imprisoning too, albeit freely chosen chains, the fetters of talent, the inhibitions of style, or learning the trade.

But there were always girls – you always kept that door open in the prison of marriage. A string of G's that year. Geneviève. Then Goldenhair, the girl of the lovely breasts on the beach, you had her out a time or two, before she was married, remembering your affair ten years gone, and how she looked on the sand, Harry. And then Geraldine. Well, who was she, except for a mouth and a laugh and a set of hours to be drinking champagne orangeades with in the garden of the Ritz, when the newly styled Caresse was away? Who was she? A girl you took in a fruit cart?

Sure. It was Paris, yes, it was August, a rich, open-necked summer. Losing money week after week on the horses, buying a bronze horse in lieu of a real one, buying etchings, buying apartments, buying friends. You never thought you were buying them – no, I know, there was never enough money it seemed – and yet other people saw only the great oil gusher of dollars, fountaining hot chocolate and brandy, leasing places to live.

So the autumn came, and you moved from the Seine and the balcony. You moved with two maids and a cook, and a governess and a chauffeur. You took an apartment in the Faubourg Saint-Honoré, with a blue-wood bathroom, and a bed built into a mirrored wall, and a carpet the grey of pearl. The wallpaper colour of rose, colour of the setting sun. The hangings green, Green for what, Harry? The green of the light moving all night from the Ritz for me, Harry. The green of corruption, the green of decay.

You were there for a year, I guess, with your home menagerie, your wife and your two kids. Not so easily to be disposed of as the two love-birds who were bought in a day and flew away, or the two white kittens who became a nuisance and were given to a little girl, or the two tortoises who were boring, and were given to a little boy. More like the two goldfish, who swam round and round in their glassy globe, and were open-eyed, and inevitable. As inevitable as the sun that rose each morning. As desired, even, almost as hated. Hated for being wanted so much.

You loved your wife, for sure. Loved the children, too, I suppose, for being a part of her. It wasn't Polly Peabody but the idea of her as Caresse that you really loved. The way she fitted into your needs, even your name – the acrostic required Mother Polly to be the malleable Caresse, the icon, the sideways bar to your sun-cross, who shared an r with you, and not much more. Someone, or something, to toss in a nightly ritual, and leave lying face up or down when you went to sleep. A thing of iron or gold, at right angles to you, and linked in the middle by nothing more than your r. Your ars, Harry. Your arse, as the English say. Your ass. Your delicious, nightly available piece of ass.

It wasn't an art you shared, really, an art of living, an art of writing, a brand of action. No, Harry, you shared a state, the state of being partners, the original all-American buddy-boy syndrome, that's what it was, for my money, the having a better hold, better, sure, when the better means nice and soft as butter, Harry, not mean and bitter. You wanted to elevate the idea of the old-fashioned love contract until it became a castle in the air, a golden fortress incised on a coin, the sovereign of the sunrise, the great male erection of the twentieth century – why, look, ladies, it's got a woman inside it, she walked right in of her own accord, she chose, goddammit, to be the princess in the tower, the snake's tongue – yes, because sometimes she turned into the mistress of venom, Harry, the spit and polish woman who scrubbed your shoes with vitriol. Was it your girls who made her so, was she jealous of your catalogue of lovers? Day by day, year by year. Did it make her sick to know she didn't even love you best? They all loved you. All those precise entries in your diary.

Like Constance Crowninshield Coolidge. You know, I

hate her with her presidential name, a name that stands for your favourite virtue, loyalty. But she wasn't loyal, was she, Harry? And she smoked as many cigarettes as you did, drank as many cocktails, bet as much – or more – on the horses. Used, later, as much or more black idol. She was your mate for a while.

Dawns of real doubting, nights of acute ecstasy. The veil drawn, and her whining voice lifted into a key of joy, a key of pain. The plan of the Castle of Love redrawn to admit of an extra room for a Queen of Pekin. By you, I mean, Harry. By you. But not by Caresse. Not then or ever. Naked home from an Arts Ball in a taxi-cab. Sure, that was one thing. Buttocks heaving in spare bedrooms when old friends from school who may have loved lion-hunters came to stay. Fine and dandy, up to a point. But a real live alternative soulfellow cum sun-worshipper locked *in situ*. Oh no. Not someone as white-thighed as Constance with now and for ever scrawled, metaphorically anyway, across her nipples. Not for Caresse. Not for Polly, baby. Polly knew when she'd had enough.

Dreams, then. Dreams. Harry tossed on his bed. Harry with chorus-girl. Harry without. Harry praying. A mystic now, it seems. Betwixt and between. And buying a dog that nobody wants. Harry in pieces. Dreams.

Of a bottomless quagmire, like the mud in the Somme, the terrible smell, the screeching sound of the shells, the sucking down, down, down, hands reaching up. Screams. Dreams. Dreams of Caresse there, Caresse reaching down. Smiling. Opening her lips in a kiss. A kiss of forgiveness.

Hatless, then. Breakfastless, coatless, Harry on the aeroplane to London. As once before, the contrite saviour from the skies - crosses the Channel, pleads his case, uses his charm, lays out all his promises. Weeps, maybe. That always helps. In moderation, or course, in moderation. And is back in the air again with a flask of Scotch and his wife tucked up in a travelling rug at his side, short skirt and all and randy again as a nutcracker.

And so you became just friends, you and Constance. Yes, just friends. In a while. It took some time, of course. A little time. But really it needn't have done. There was never a chance, you see, Harry, was there. You couldn't leave Caresse, you told her. You could, though. Oh yes, I think you could. But that wasn't the point. Not when you heard that Constance wouldn't marry you, anyway. Not when she said she was going to marry someone else. The Comte de Jumilhac. Wow. That must have been a shock, Harry. After those afternoons in the pink marble bath. Male pride being what it is. Yours most of all. The Comte de Jumilhac. A Frenchman. An aristocrat. And, yes, another thing. He used to have a saying. How did it go, Harry? Remind me. Yes, that's it. 'If you don't want to be a pigeon, you have to be a shark.'

Sure, Harry. It must have been hard to take. It must have been real hard.

Forget it, Harry. You can hear the foghorn sounding from the quay. The guard has already put the whistle in his mouth. The aircrews are turning. The voyage is over. You keep coming back up to me, Harry, but you can't give a girl as much whisky as I had and expect her to knife her legs round your naked waist. The way you like so much. The way you told me once Caresse did the day you made love on the grave. Lying back in the winter sun. On the mossy slab. In the Cimetière de l'Abbaye de Longchamp. Smiling up at you. Pulling her skirt up over her knees. Hearing the old crone ringing her bell to close the gates.

'Hurry up,' she said. 'There's not much time.' 'I don't know,' you said, fiddling with your trouser buttons. Wanting it then and there. Loving the very idea. The girl on the grave. The act in the cemetery. The yielding flesh on the cold autumn stone. 'Come on, Harry. Hurry up. There's time.' Her hands working the skirt up. Over her stocking-tops. The thighs moving. Lace pretties. Black on the skin. Silk on the stone. Her hands under the elastic, sliding them down. Her buttocks rising to let them pass. Oh Christ. You were on

79

to her then, seeing, out of the corner of your eye, a white goat browsing under the wall, a leaning tombstone to your left with a splendid urn balanced as if to topple the moment you came.

You came, Harry. Death amidst life, sex amidst stones. You lay on that ancient miserable stone and you vowed you'd be buried there, the two of you, both in the one grave with the old woman ringing her bell to let visitors in and out, and the goat cropping the grass, and the great sea of overgrown vegetation everywhere, the tangled undergrowth of eternity, the tumbling stones, the urns and the chains, the rusted railings, the flaking words, frost on the ground and dead leaves, the air cold and damp and the falling crosses, and the grave of the king's dancer, and moss on the walls, and the cyclamen. And you and Caresse, the pair of you, settled into your niche in the cold unchanging stone.

You kept going back. Once to read Oscar Wilde there, learning the rules of how to obey your own instincts with Dorian Gray as your guide. The same as it was in Turin, lying with Caresse in a hot bath. Remembering the circular bath-tub that once belonged to Marie-Louise, with its grilled gate, and the pink marble bath on the Quai d'Orsay you washed with Constance in. You were never one to reserve a treat for a single person, Harry. Your cemetery became the precious secret you shared with us all. The heat and movement of water, the chill and stability of stone. The sea and the grave, these were your symbols, that year. Bubble baths, and marble slabs.

And then it was 1924, the year you made your black-tie decision. Bored by politics, and seeing life as an affair of imperial souls. Always to wear a black tie, no doubt in mourning. For what? The state of the world. Or my own then still unknown and still long to be cherished virginity. Soaping the parts down there with my eyes closed. Not knowing what was to become. Going to come. Or who. Or when.

You bought a racehorse. You decided to go hatless, losing

your hat. You raced your horse, Bucentaur, and it lost. You lay with Caresse each night rolling dice to decide which side of the bed to sleep on. You stole a skull from the catacombs. You were photographed with your father holding it.

Your father, Harry. This was the year he wrote to criticise your ambition to be a poet. This was the year you met your surrogate father – well, was he that, I wonder? – your friend and mentor, anyway, your admired and cynical, elderly, aristocratic and handsome Walter Berry, connoisseur of books, and lover of women. As Boston, in certain ways, as they come. Iconoclast, in others. A supercilious eye on a spear of pride. He admired your guts, Harry, he shared your taste in women. He liked Caresse.

Days, then, you spent, there in his elegant room with the little Degas nude you wanted to make love to, handling his Burne-Jones, and his prayer shell from Tibet, and his Aztec death mask, and his vast, almost pathologically vast, collection of books, books eaten by rats, books abandoned in rain, books bound – or at least one book bound – in the skin of a prostitute. They made a luxurious feast for your hungry soul, Harry. Starving for Baudelaire, glutted on erotica, listing the words that stirred you.

It passed, that year. A dull year. Under the shadow of losing Constance. Finding with Caresse in America, the occasional other. A Blanche – who rhymed with avalanche – a Mademoiselle Fragile at the races, an Italian model who posed in the nude. You wore your wife's knickers, you sent rude cables. You were yourself.

Look at me, Harry. This is the truth. In 1923 you began to perceive what it was. The intimate, indissoluble connection between love and death. For you, at least. For you, for always. There in the Cimetière de l'Abbaye de Longchamp, while the seasons turned the sun burned down out of a cloudless sky, and the great leaves of the planes fluttered in the October wind, and the flakes of snow gathered in the lips of the urns, in the morning when the sweepers were out with their brooms, and in the evening when the shadows tipped the railings with a jetty ink, at high noon under the mourning statues, and mid-way through the afternoon reclined on the rim of a tomb with a volume of poems, alone sometimes, even, but usually with Caresse or a friend, you began to resolve your doubts into one overriding purpose, the need to select the hour of your own demise, and to garland this with an act of love, and to feel truly happy doing so, and to see this conjunction as the right and true end of living.

And so, Harry. It came to this.

Twelve

Six years after the end of the war. That was the year of the sun for you, the year of the strike against all that your upbringing in Boston meant, the long skirts laid aside and the flappers showing their knees, the parasols torn into ribbons, the invention of sun-glasses. But not for you, Harry. You hated whatever opticians had to be doing for you, for ordinary vision or against the blinding light. You set your eyes on the dark centre.

In 1925, you started to tan your skin to the Indian red you always keep it now. A camel voyage across the African sand in the heart of winter, quitting Europe in frost and snow, moving beside Caresse on the white Sahara Express to the end of the line, to where the caravan would begin, at Touggourt. Oh yes, I see you there. The spoiled rich young American couple the world is going to have to get to know a lot better, touring the globe with their good suitcases, their wad of dollars, and their fresh, so endlessly fresh opinions, open-eyed and open-ended, ready for anything, anything, sure, so long as it isn't everyday, or smells of Boston, or makes you feel cold.

You had a fine entourage, Harry. The guide who spoke American – some of it, anyway – the valet-cum-cook in a Palm Beach suit and a red fez and dancing pumps, the eternal Arab with his eye on the West the way you had yours on the south. Then the camel-keeper with two fine sons to help him drive, and, for good measure, a flute player and a tom-tom drummer, and last of all but by no means least, watch out for more news in this space, the belly-dancer, little Zora, virginal thirteen. Eight servants there for a three-day canter along a series of low dunes. Back in time for the train, and all perfectly safe – like so much in your life, until today, Harry, it only seemed wild.

How much did it cost, Harry? How many green dollars – green, they tell us, and why? Because the Jews pick them before they're ripe – how many Moroccan or Tunisian or French whatever they were did it cost you to buy eight souls and a change of camels? To sail west as if on a great spongy liner with beautiful supercilious eyebrows, and see the sun, and admire the moon lavender-luscious and later arctic, and hear the slow low keening of the two musicians out in the darkness beyond the tents. You lay together wrapped like cocoons in your two white burnouses, two of you, yes, and a third not far away, and less far still in your mind, Harry, the little voluminous-petticoated Zora, still a friend, only a friend and the stimulating memory of her belly rolling, slowly, voluptuously, to fuel your night in the arms of Caresse.

How much did it cost you? How many hours of dreaming, lying awake with your hands under your head, and hearing the jackals howl? Tasting the aftermath of the camel's milk – an aphrodisiac mixed, they said, with honey – and fingering, maybe, yes, the four jars of the best brand of opium you had bought in Tunis, but never opened yet, never used, but would do soon. How many hours? How many miles on the bumping, swaying backs of your ships of the desert, many and ruminant? How many miles on the sweltering train thinking of Biskra, wondering what they would say to three people sharing a two-bed room in the best hotel? How many doubts about what Caresse would say when you asked her – Say, shall we take little Zora home, shall we ask her to sleep with us?

Under the sun, under the frost in the morning, burying things in the sand. A bronze medallion first with your sun-cross, and then – bizarre as ever, Harry – two self-addressed postcards to your new apartment in Paris, written in white on the first occasion you ever smoked in a hashish den. The pipes passed in the sound of keening instruments, before the sword dancing, and then the gyrations again, the spins of Zora becoming the very turns of the world, layers upon layers of clothes unleafing – Oh, plump Caresse, are you grieving, over little Zora unleaving into a dark alleyway and up the stairs, convulsive shiverings, and then three in a bed, and earrings upon her ears and bracelets upon her hands? How much did it cost, Harry? How much did it cost in fear, how much in loss of trust, this need for a stripping of onion skins to the very core of propriety, the bare belly of shared and virginal ecstasy? I wonder.

Was it Zora who gave you the need for tattoos? Were there snakes and sun rays in the flesh around her groin, in the private places the public never saw, in the secret areas of her soul? An Arab in Biskra, lacking skill, gave you a cross on the sole of your foot. Later in Paris, leaning over the Pont Royal, you saw a man on a barge, and tattooed across his back a knight astride a charger holding a spear, and you wanted more. You wanted lions and gazelles, the sun and slave-girls, the exotic incised symbolic impedimenta of a great civilisation obsessed with glory and images, a sort of pagan bible in pictures engraved on your own skin, the imagination of a Baudelaire in blue needle-imprinted majesty on your breast and your arms.

So the year wore on, governed by Baudelaire and laudanum – the poison to kill yourself with – and you went one day to the grave of Baudelaire and the tomb of Wilde, and you bought a racehorse that died in training, and another that ran and ran and ran again and never won. Betting, running yourself, having others now run for you, horses and other poets. You formed your style, Harry, a drab style, the boring chime upon chime of your early sonnets, the fourteen-line

clumping clamping things you began to feel showed a trace
of your master, the man of the flowers of evil.

Running, then, like your horses, in a tough race. You
wrote for the master – a sonnet for Baudelaire's birthday.
You wrote one for the war, remembering the men and the
wire, the shells and the mud, and you found a pair of your
best lines till then, clogging some good words, like crawling
and cringing and sucking mire, in the awful surge of the
drear pentameter, echoing Alan Seeger more than Baudelaire
there, Harry.

Caresse, too. Caresse ageing, Caresse those crucial years
older, nursing her lovely breasts, visiting studios and learning to paint, looking for something to do, something to be,
Caresse, too, was a sonneteer, and an earlier one than you
were. 1925, the year Zora danced, Caresse wrote. Flesh into
rhythm, flesh into words.

How do you see my flesh, Harry, still as it is now in death?
Bend over. Yes. Lower. There. Can you see the secret under
the lids of my eyes, the waxen moment arriving when even I,
your final priestess, have to leave you behind in the waiting-
room of eternity? Listen. Do you hear a fly buzz as I die? Or
am I alive still, in a sense? Yes, in a sense, Harry. Think a
moment. What can you do with a once beautiful, still
attractive, fully clothed and presentable young woman.

Undress me, Harry. Sure. Go on. Take off my clothes.
Pull up the shoes over my stiff toes. Good. Very good. Now
stroke the stockings. Mmmm. What a silken scrackle. Pull
up the skirt. Go on. Further. Further. No one can stop you
now. Not even me. I'm not even here, really. I'm just a
memory in the air, about a foot above the hole in my
forehead, I'd say. Watching. Smiling. Yes, I agree. A little
excited, maybe just a little, at the thought of having the
stockings drawn off my dead legs, and your warm hands
feeling their way over my cold thighs.

Unlatch the suspender belt. Use both hands. Draw them
down, lifting my legs, yes, one at a time. Why, there. You
have one, gauzy-fine as a dragonfly, in your fingers. Empty

86

sheath of a once pretty girl. Your girl, Harry. Your Josephine. Go on, now. Run your hand up her thigh. Look in her eyes. She won't look back, she's pretending she doesn't notice. She keeps her eyes on the same point all the time, a point about four feet from the ceiling. You see, that's where I'm floating. Waiting. Waiting for you to fire the second shot.

So what are you waiting for? Are you going to strip me naked, Harry? Have a bare corpse on the bed, yourself clothed, or naked here by my side? You can do what you like, you know. You can touch me wherever you want. You can do what you never dared, maybe, even you, Harry, to ask for when I was alive. You can have it all. Lady Suicide grants her Lord her life. But remember. The future will take your measure by what you do. You have to keep that in mind. You have to be careful. Your obituary is here on my skin.

Thirteen

Downstairs then. Take a look in the mirror first, though. Don't allow yourself to forget it's the face of a murderer you are seeing, Harry, unless you come back. Unless you come back as you promised, and join me. Straighten your tie. Sure. It looks good as it is. A bit awry. The sweet disorder in the dress, eh? How about that, Harry? I'm getting the knack at last of being a literary girl? Okay. So leave your black gardenia the way it is, and your hair messed. I like it that way.

So often, Harry, your colour was black. Black, then. Say a prayer to black now, put your hands together and let me hear the clap of silence for the crackling black of winter, the still familiar bombazine black of funeral stiffness. Now, Harry. Now.

As then. The day you gave away your brown suit and swore, and wrote the entry for April 17th, 1926, in your diary, and often repeated the vow, even to me, that you would from thence forward always wear dark blue – the nearest to black you could reasonably get, I suppose – and tie a black knitted necktie and put a black artificial gardenia in your buttonhole and go bareheaded, scorching black in the sun.

There were races every day a short run from Paris; every month from February to December, except August, you could lay your money on horses at Longchamp, or at Chantilly, or at Auteuil, even – to redeem the blank month of August – on the coast at Deauville. You took your opportunity, Harry, followed your dream. Whatever it was, dream or addiction, or simply, sometimes, the daily habit, the outcome of boredom – let's go to the races, okay, your car or mine, let's go – you would ride out with the Count or some other friend, aristocrat, or pauper, and risk your francs.

Black. Still in the black, though. After nights of clever calculation, fiddling the figures into some new pattern, admitting some fresh allowance for training or travel or tickets or treats, you would find that the overall amount expended, lost and won, still kept your account afloat, in the black, sure. Never, not ever, in the red. This was your black year, Harry, your year of discovering darkness to be a colour, funereal man as you now were in your suit of deepest blue.

Something Egyptian perhaps was beginning. Something aware of a ritual and a dynasty of dying, a darkness, emphasised by the slashed lining showing the heart of the sun, a fine orange, or a dim scarlet, something exemplified in the lean head of the whiphound body of the God Seth, whippet-lean, Harry-black, everlasting in brooding awareness of life passing and racing colours going into the night.

So you bought Narcisse Noir. I see him there in the photograph you showed me taken at Deauville on the sands, you standing erect in your dark suit with a woman on either side of you – Caresse here, your sister there, and the dog at your feet, a long coil of black like a panther, like something so dark it must have fallen through your trousers out of your own black groin, and curled, snout low, like a sexual principle inhibited by the lens of the camera obscura, muscular flesh and bone over dark shoes.

Narcisse Noir. So black he seemed to look at himself in a deep, undying pool of perpetual blackness, too black to return an image of his own colour. So fast he could outrun his own shadow. So lean he could disappear when you looked at him sideways, like a silhouette in profile. Your alter ego, Harry. Your own black dog melancholy, taken out of your dark soul and thrown on to a screen.

Over fourteen hectic days, you raced him. Losing the Prix Beau-Soleil – was there ever a day you lost the trail of the beautiful sun – by a whisker, a mere nothing, winning the Prix Coram, racing, racing, then two in one day, winning the second from scratch, and he had beaten Lynes and Castellane, and he was the best. I see you lifting a foaming glass of champagne, or maybe a Black Russian for this one, draining it off, tipping a drop on the poor dog's ear for a prize libation. Harry Crosby, dog-owner.

Going to the dogs. Gone to the dogs. You made him a partner in your most intimate ceremonies. He lay across the bed while you slept, his toenails lacquered with gold. He travelled first-class to the USA, padding the deck without a lead, spring-heeled in the lilt of the waves, never sea-sick, licking the hands that fed him, eating caviar and potatoes, drinking whisky sours from a trough in the Vaudeville Bar. He was everybody's friend, a quicksilver addition to any party, barking with joy to hear the glasses chink and see the lampshade dresses flirt in the Black Bottom.

Night after night you took him round the woods of Paris, exercising his long legs over stone or wet grass, running yourself to keep him in sight, halting and calling, waiting when you were outrun, authority smitten, panting, learning to whistle, wanting him back. And then seeing him turn, sniff the air, and come headlong lickety-split across the grass again, or the road, ignoring traffic, letting the horns shriek and the brakes squeal in rage, eager to reach his master, his black alternative, his human consort, you, Harry.

He was your dog, that is, your spirit. Not the first. The year before you had bought a mongrel hound, named him Corydon. He took to swallowing his own shit, like all dogs, and you felt an affinity with him there, too, calling him dung-devourer, as you were a sun-devourer.

Narcisse Noir was luckier. Yes. You showed me the

photograph of his mistress and mate, the one you flew to London for, and named Clytoris, white in her hide as he was black, and warmed by a felt coat, since she always seemed to shiver and feel the cold. I understand how she felt, poor little bitch. It was cold that year in Venice. Cold when I saw you bringing Narcisse Noir along to our evening walk, under the Bridge of Sighs. He had on an iron muzzle, by law. No Clytoris for him. No love-bites.

More than one might have said for you, Harry, pacing beside me along the dank canals, nibbling my ear, hearing the sound of the water dripping from a lifted car, or the notes deliquescing from a fallen serenade, and the dog whining. Whining on. Whining on. I came to hate the silly brute, those days, and was glad when you saw how it was and hired a dog-minder. Day after day Narcisse Noir was walked by a doorman in uniform, and with white gloves, who stopped and looked at the sky while he shat.

Were your other girls so fussy, Harry? Did they all hate to have dog-turds discovered under their mattresses, fouling their best shoes, urine that stank of race-courses impregnating their underclothes if they left them lying on the floor? Did they all hate, as I did, the endless moaning and yearning whenever the dog was locked in another room, and heard the first expectorant throating gasping sounds of his master's orgasm? It always put me off, Harry.

Yes, I remember Narcisse Noir. The Black Narcissus always left in the bath-tub whenever I went for a shower. Limping out of the clean porcelain with a guilty, reproachful look, and a pair of disgustingly dirty paws. Always there on the sofa, leaving hairs, whenever I wanted a rest, or even to change my stockings. There too, rubbing his thin red thing on the back of my calves, if I leant forward.

Lewd. Like the gross underbelly of your own excited love, Harry. I hated that dog. I wanted once to put rat poison into his tray of biscuits and watch him squirm into quick extinction. Yes. I can say that now. I'm beyond needing to watch my words, Harry. I've won through to the last licence. The right to be honest given only to those who die.

So listen. I'll tell you about your dog. About your obsession with blackness, and running. The treacle syndrome, let's call it. Your need to have something with you always to represent the antithesis of the bright sun, some ashes to match the flame in your cigarette lighter. It stinks, Harry. It really does. Like your dog. Like your girl.

Yes, Harry, like your girl will, too. And rather soon. And you, too. And this whole damn filthy flat of Mortimer's where we've had our final fuck. I know. I'm growing coarse as I rot. I feel the words get rougher the moment they rise to my lips. I feel like a white bitch myself, another Clytoris in my winter coat, in case I shiver. So let me finish, Harry. Not in Venice, after the Lido, kissing the dog farewell by the vaporetto stage, when you were so near to tears at losing me I took pity and tried to let you see I was nice, and I might come back, and, look, Harry, I even love your dog.

No, not then, but in Boston. City of Dreadful Night, 1926 again. Harry at home in Beacon Street, up in the attic, secretly into the Chinese Room. Contemplating water bombs again. And alone. Except for. Yes. Why not? So up he comes, quietly dragged on a lead, nobody seeing, the final outrage, the dog let into the house's most perfect room, to lie on the Aubusson rug, smear the Japanese canopies with his greasy sides. And there, black on black lacquer, as Japanese and inscrutable as the orient embroidered on lilac, a snake of a dog on a golden dragon let into the floor, let disappear for ever, dark as Egypt, into the musty recesses of old Boston. A hidden insult. A buried reproach. This animal in with the porcelain. A final Harry nose-thumbing at all he most hates in whatever he comes from. Things in their place, dogs in their kennels. The sun out of reach in the sky, darkness at night.

So be it. The kiss, a true kiss, for Narcisse Noir.

Fourteen

Who will it be, though? I mean, who do you think Caresse will ask to come up to this room and examine our two bodies? Because, you know, she'll never come herself. She's afraid. Not of your own face with a hole in the back of it smeared with grey from the fire of the shot. Not that. No. She's afraid of the other woman. Of finding me, Josephine, here, me with a smile on my face and your free arm around my shoulder the way you plan to arrange it the second you pull the trigger.

She'll never come. She'll pretend it was just you here, you see if she doesn't. She'll go through the rest of her life swearing you died alone. But she'll know, really. Even if no one tells her, or shows her the newspapers, she'll know. Inside her head, she'll know. So she'll send a trusted friend, Harry. Someone who knows how to keep his mouth shut, a reserved, sensible man. Someone like – yes – like Archibald MacLeish.

You were going to see him tomorrow, weren't you, Harry. You and Caresse. Drink a gin fizz or two together before he went back to Massachusetts to his farm. You'll see, she'll send MacLeish. A long streak of puritanical Scottish disapproval to sit up all night and examine our – no, Harry, just your by then, maybe – your body. What will he do, I wonder? Will he come up here first, and identify you? Well, I

93

guess he'll have to. Someone will. The way Albert will have to come and identify me.

Poor Albert. He'll never understand how it was. Whatever they say, it will seem like murder most foul to Albert. Sure, he'll read all the evidence, and he'll see the smile on my face, and he'll draw the only conclusion. I went to my death all unsuspecting. Yes. With a smile on my face. Never expecting this nice man with a black gardenia in his buttonhole to pull out a – what? A penis? A pistol? 'Good God, man, if she'd ever thought he was going to kill her, don't you think she'd have shown the fact on her face?'

Poor Albert. Yes. He'll get a bad shock. I don't believe he'll get over it all his born days. He'll go to the grave supposing Harry Crosby to have tried to rape his dear and loving wife, who resisted, and was shot for her loyalty. Well maybe you did, in your way, Harry. Maybe you did. We had a rough passage that first time in the sand on the Lido, however much I enjoyed it. Yes. There was blood to be wiped away. More than once. I liked that. You know I liked to be hurt. They say that women never do but I know I did then.

So, Harry. Picture the scene. The policemen filling the room with their big boots and their powder for fingerprints. And the doctor, pacing up and down, with his black bag on a chair here by the bed. This chair with the cane seat, the one my arm keeps trailing over. And, yes. The door opening, and the two of them coming in. Together, maybe. MacLeish for you, and Albert for me. To identify who we are. Like witnesses for a wedding. But only you have the ring, Harry. The sun ring. The one Caresse gave you and which you always wear on your finger.

Wore. Sure. Okay. Rip it off. Stamp it into the floor. Flatten it out. Forget the ring. Forget the fact that you've had to choose to be here with *me* when you die. Forget the world, Harry. Just let your mind fix close in on what you have time left to do. Like picture the look on MacLeish's face when he sees the pair of us here on the bed. You dead. A friend, and the husband of a friend.

I liked him, Harry. I liked the way he walked, the way he talked, the way he had of chewing the cud of his thoughts like a wise old Scottish cow. Fought in the war, later resigned from his law practice. The perfect model for what the prospective writer, or so you thought, Harry, ought to aim to do. And he wrote well. 'Jesus, wincingly well,' I remember you telling me. 'Too well for comfort, Josephine. Too well to beat, I guess.' Which was when you quoted the bit about the sun. 'Enter the stars. And here face down beneath the sun. And here upon earth's noonward height. To feel the always coming on. The always rising of the night.' You went right through it in the little market place, turning over the mauve glass in your fingers, tracing the lines on the stem, it seemed, eager to make me see, to make me love them, the way you did yourself. Lines from a hero. Lines from the greatest – after Eliot, of course – of all living modern poets, Archibald MacLeish, American and genius.

Then you went through the whole poem, by heart, screwing up your eyes behind the lenses, head up squinting at the sun for inspiration, from Ecbatan to Kermanshah to Palmyra, the air flashing with the landward gulls over Sicily, the low pale light across the land, like Swinburne only modern, the long light on the sea, like John Masefield, only not a Brit. You threw the names out, the comparisons, as you quoted, making me see, Harry, making me want to share it with you, the long bleak rush of the sun dying, the terrible surge towards annihilation no one, you thought, had ever caught so well. 'It's nihilism, Josephine,' you said. 'Nihilism. It leaves no hope, and it's so damn good. "And here face downward in the sun. To feel how swift, how secretly. The shadow of the night comes on." The very opposite,' you said, 'of what I believe.' Looking up still, dazzled and fascinated, right into the eye of the Venice sun there in the market-place. Your God, Harry. Your bright Apollo.

'I'm going to beat him, Josephine,' you said. 'I'm going to

95

bring the sun back. The way it comes back every day, right plumb from the centre of the sea, red and squalling, a new-born babe of light in the fog of dawn. I'm going to be the poet of the sun the way MacLeish is the poet of darkness. Give me time. That's all I ask. A little time.' Oh, Harry. You were pretty then. You were really pretty. Blond above dark sunburned skin. A young Apollo yourself going out to do battle against those forces of darkness, Hector against the Achilles of night. The sun's champion.

At Gstaad. Skiing. You and Caresse. Suddenly two other smiling big American men, breath making white clouds in the air, leaning on sticks, gloved, stiff and plump in their ski clothes, heads in wool hats, goggles up, their eyes on Caresse's breasts.

Then talking. Not the thin one, maybe. Not MacLeish, with his taciturn reserved manner, his polite Scotsman's reticence, his towering stooped frame. No, the other one spoke, I guess. Reserved, maybe, too. But fondling the dog, showing the way all animals took to him. Showing his masculinity and his tenderness, one eye on the dog, really on the dog, one left for Caresse. Yes, the eye of a man about to leave his wife, with another woman lined up and waiting, and yet speculating, comparing, keeping the field in view for a crazy moment, able and ready to turn any which way he chose, licensed to screw, Harry.

Remember Ernest. 'The trouble is,' MacLeish told you, 'that Ernest is too wrapped up in the importance of being Ernest. The importance, one might indeed say, of being *earnest* – even a little *too* earnest sometimes – about Ernest. He cares passionately about the English, you see. The aristocratic ones, that is. The rest he loathes. He met a colonel once in Turkey who had his whole vocabulary reduced to a hundred words. He talked exactly the way Ernest wanted to write. He never exaggerated. He was never at a loss for what to say. He said everything just as it was. I loved that goddam guy. They shot his legs off the day they killed the horses in the river.

'Ernest,' MacLeish told you, 'has a strange sense of

humour. And the whole of American prose,' he added, 'is going to be remodelled in the image of that inarticulate and, alas, legless British colonel in Turkey. You see, Harry,' he told you, bony-browed above his whisky sour, 'we are dealing here with a genius. The greatest prose writer since the death of Henry James.'

Grace, Harry. 'Grace under pressure. That's what he thinks,' MacLeish told you. 'Courage is grace under pressure.' You have to show it now, whether you want to or not. And it's going to put you ahead of the game. Ernest, for sure. And maybe some of the others. Whatever they say in public, they're going to know you put your life on the line. You came through with the goods. You put the gun to your head the same way as Dr Hemingway senior did last year in Oak Park, Chicago. The sun sets, Harry. But the sun also rises. You're going to be there in the history books for all time because of that little hole in the back of your head.

1926, *The Sun Also Rises*, Ernest's first novel. It sold fast. As Ernest rose, hitting the best-seller lists and holding the top against all comers the year (was it only this year, Harry) *A Farewell to Arms* came out. So there he is, there he was, fourteen stone of blood and muscle and sheer talent frowning down at you on the ski slope at Gstaad, fondling your dog, lusting after your wife, ready to drink you under the table. The man with the phrase of hope, the man beside him with the words of annihilation. American genius personified, and set there thus two-headed, one for verse and one for prose, hunched in a pair of padded uniforms on a skid of solid ice in Switzerland.

I'll bet you wished you'd thought of Ecclesiastes first, Harry. *The Sun Also Rises*. It gave the lie to those great lines of MacLeish's, it set the reign of darkness back a peg. It showed you the way to go. The road – oh, sure – you were on already, Harry, the road out through the sun setting and round the back to the following day and the dawn red there like always against the black horizon.

Somehow you never cared for prose. That was why you

97

saw Ernest only as a great guy, a fine drinker, as a man willing to waste, for a while, for a price, as many days at the races as you were. He gave you a photograph of an arm taken whole from the belly of a shark, he introduced you (or maybe MacLeish did) to Joyce. To Joyce. The one you really wanted to know, who wrote the kind of prose that Rimbaud might have wanted, if he'd ever written a novel.

No, there was something cool about Ernest. Almost cold. Calculating. He lacked the kind of heart you wanted to pluck out and offer bleeding to the sun. You saw the grace, but maybe you doubted the pressure. Or maybe you just had the old East Coast suspicion of any society boy coming in from the Mid-West the way Fitzgerald has. I know your madness, Harry. You've worked the way Hemingway has, in your own manner, but you need a myth, too. And you'll pay the price. Sure you will.

MacLeish won't like this, Harry. He isn't the type to feel a thrill. He'll have a long safe life, that one, and die in his bed, full of years, full of fame. So he'll give you your vigil, not in the way of a man enjoying, really, a nasty job that's fallen to him, but out of duty only, and to please Caresse. You dumb bastard, I can hear him thinking. You poor dumb bastard. Arranging his chair so he can't see the hole in your head. Reflecting on life and literature, and the awful things that occur when the two mix.

Not so Ernest, Harry. Don't worry. You have your heir there. He'll make the usual noises, the way the rest will. But it won't be the same. He'll feel the thrill. The strange throb in his heart to know a man who went through with a shooting. Laid his life on the board and let the slicer come down. Pure bacon. Pure sensation. And then he'll forget. And then he'll remember. And then one day. You'll see, Harry. You won't be the only American writer who puts a gun to his head and blows his brains out. You're starting a fashion, boy. Roll up and take your aim.

Fifteen

Publication. Everyone wants to see his name in lights, in print, on the cover of a book, across the front of a theatre, somewhere out beyond the privacy of a letter or a diary, Harry, somewhere a stranger might see and know it. So you walked the streets, the pair of you, you and Caresse, a couple of young sonneteers in search of a publisher. Here and there. There and here.

And you found. Yes. The very man. In a tiny shop on a twisting street near St Germain-des-Prés. Squinting over the typeface for a flowery advertisement or a wedding announcement in a local paper. The master printer. Self-styled. M. Roger Lescaret. He could smell the money, I guess. The French have a nose for who can pay, and he probably sized up the price of Caresse's jewels the moment you walked in through the door, jangling the old rusting bells, and looking round like a film director inspecting a set.

He could work, though. You took an ageing jobbing printer – oh, he was never a master anything, Harry, not before he met you and Caresse – and you got him enthusiastic enough to print some of the loveliest folios of the 1920s. On rich paper you could eat your dinner off. And in bindings a connoisseur could spend a lifetime stroking. Look. This English book from the Bodley Head. I can see you, Harry, leaning over his dusty shoulder, flattening out the exquisite

Nonesuch Donne on his crowded work table. I want you to copy that, M. Lescaret. As a specimen. To give us an idea of your style.

So he concentrated, and in five days he had produced not only a copy, but the beginnings of a design of his own. He had flair. You were both enchanted. Hands clapping, glasses produced. Champagne corks popping, and a splendid liaison forged amidst the fonts of type and the stacks of provincial newspapers.

Out they came, the first five books. A new press was named after that slender hound: Éditions Narcisse. But then the sun crept in and the press took its name from its master: the Black Sun Press.

You were upstairs by then, selecting titles at a leather-topped bureau in a corner beside a window, with Caresse near at your elbow shuffling type and shades of leather. A pair of publishers. A day or two a week. Allowing yourselves the luxury of seeming to be employed – it made a good story for a letter home to Boston – and acquiring a way of handing out a donation to those you thought were deserving, and didn't like the idea of charity. Well. That's the curse of the rich, Harry. The cross that comes with being one of the rich, Harry. The cross that comes with being one of the four hundred.

More than that, though. You had your outlet for your own poems, your own prose. *Red Skeletons* was on the streets, in the bookshops, in private hands, on reviewers' desks, even in Boston, within two months of your finding your *maître imprimeur*. At home you had the skeleton of a girl you'd bought from an antique dealer clanking and rattling above the stairs. At work you had your second collection of sonnets rasping and creaking in the ice and blood of a nasty Paris winter.

Illustrated, too. That was really the point, I suppose. It was Alastair – Baron Hans Henning – whose drawings you chose. You were half beyond your Baudelaire phase, Harry, by the time the book was arranged in type, with seventeen poems about the sun written in free verse. This was your new vehicle, Harry, your chariot of the sun. And they came out flapping their wings like golden eagles all that year, in the stamp of Rimbaud. You had a new idol, and you rode him hard.

The sonnets were looking back already, the day they hit the streets. All decadence and a breath of the 1890s exfoliating in suicide and grey fogs and girls you missed in the tone of Arthur Symons - I'm really good on the names, Harry, now aren't I? Or maybe it was simply Lionel Johnson imitating Shakespeare. Well? It was all gold and fire and rush and madness and trying your hand at symbolism and scrapping rhymes and learning how to be modern and get away with murder and be as new as MacLeish or Eliot or Cummings.

In the Baron you found your man. An artist more extreme, it seems, than the most death-obsessed of the followers of Burne-Jones. And as linear, and reproducible, so you quickly saw, as the divine Aubrey – thin women in black with cigarette holders as long as canes, men with goat's legs and top-hats, castles that spired up into sexual pinnacles topped with rainbows and dragonflies, a landscape of whirling clouds and fiery bushes, weather that simmered and flushed the steeples of grotesque places of worship, minor distant villages made gross with unnameable vices hinted at in the horns of pigs, the genitalia of bullocks, the festering buds of trees littering the ground with acorns or severed limbs.

You and Caresse found his mansion near Versailles amidst the dripping firs, an enchanted palace as weird as anything drawn by his own dripping scalpel. Surrounded, you later thought, by a fringe of grim larches, and echoing to the music of bats and owls. Wherein, upon the door being opened by a black footman, in a suit of black livery, you were both conducted through corridors lit only by candles and hung with louche cartoons into a smoky cavernous drawing room almost empty of furniture – across the polished floor of which there suddenly skated the white satin-clad figure of a strange gnome, of, it seemed, advanced age, who did the splits, rose, bowed and seized you by the hand, imparting a moist kiss to the back of your wrist. It ought to have been a sign. But he was subtle. He kissed your wife, as well.

A genius of penmanship, and an unreliable friend. He showed you the edge, Harry. The point beyond which you felt you didn't want to go. It seemed, very soon, that you spoke to each other across a gulf of atrocious plans, many too outré even for you to consider enacting. For Alastair there was only the bizarre. Decay and corruption pleased him as much as death and violence, possibly more. He had an eye and a nose for the stench of pollution, the glittering petrol-sweet odour of things rotting.

At first, it fascinated. Later, it cloyed. You were already caught by the sun, and Alastair's black imagination arrived, really, too late. You gave him work. You dedicated *Red Skeletons* to him, and his bony horrors illuminated the more shocking implications of those drear verses. They peered out through a network, a trellis, of Alastair's visions, his delirium of pederasty and Sodom.

You grew close. Closer than you, Harry, with your still unawaked interest in men, would have wanted. Less close than Alastair, who was now in love, might have wanted. A pass was made, no doubt. On a clean lawn in the Bois. Or behind a case of books in a library, eyeing a lewd manuscript together. Or walking through rain beneath an umbrella at Calais. Or lying smoking opium slithering against each other in a mound of D'Annunzian cushions. Below the great wheel of fire in the cathedral at Chartres, perhaps, staring up at the sun's flamboyance corroding in stone, you felt a thin hand on your waist, lower maybe, a subtly reaching finger, an old man's — as it must have been to you, Harry — despicable lustfulness groping for what you had never offered, an intimacy, a sharing of bodily thrust. And you withdrew. Shocked? Scarcely. But irritated, no doubt. And anxious to put a little more distance between your skin and Alastair's passion.

Letters were exchanged. There were quarrels, misunderstandings. You were never prudish, Harry, but Alastair could make you seem so.

So remember. That day this year when you took the eighty unsold copies of *Red Skeletons* you had left, and stacked up a bonfire, and threw on paraffin, and stood back, and lit the pyre, and watched the title-page curl and take the flame, and the word Alastair, your dedicatee, char and blacken and die away, eighty times, until you felt finally cleansed, of him, and of all the foulness the book still brought to mind. I know. You wrote to me. And I understand.

'When the fire died,' you told me, 'there were still four copies left, half smouldering, and not likely to catch and blaze, because it was starting to rain. So I went and got my revolver, the one with the sun on the butt' – the very one you put back in your pocket an hour ago, Harry, the very one you're going to have to take out and use again very soon – 'and I shot the last four copies full of holes. And then I felt better, really better. Clean again.

'So much for Alastair. So much for figs and mad women and dwarves and things going bad. I want the sun now. The blazing orb in the sky of possibility, the genius of the future, the herald of optimism, the golden charger. I want to be all flame, Josephine. And you are the Fire Princess to make me so. The green and orange at the heart of the flame. The startling evocation of sun in action. The chance to be young again.'

Was I, Harry? I wonder. I hope I was. I hope I am still. Do I still seem young here on the slipping coverlet, with the flies buzzing, and my skirt mussed, and the bullet-hole – the ever present, inescapable bullet-hole – in the white of my forehead, Harry? Tell me now. Tell me true. Do I still seem young? Still the gateway to the sun? Still the fresh draught of pure yolk from the golden goose's egg you wanted? I want to know, Harry. I want to know if it really seems worth while.

But I guess I'll never know. Never. Not now. Even if I ever could have done. You see, you have to die to find out how much people really care for you. And then it's too late. I wish it wasn't, Harry. But it is. I know it is.

Sixteen

You can dream, Harry. Dream that your pipe is here, and the black idol simmering away over the flame. Dream, yes. But the facts are just that you're here alone with me and there isn't any opium, Harry, and no pipe either, and only a dreg or two in the bottom of the bottle of Cutty Sark to solace your troubles.

You were never happy when someone else described the boundaries. You were the one to lay down the rules, or you got excited, and lost your temper, and sulked. So dream, Harry. Dream. Dip the bamboo stick in the bowl, ease out a piece of the sticky opium, twist it over the fine point like the bonfire toffee you used to be given at Hallowe'en, watch it roasting there, like the stinking fleece from a goat, over the blue flame, slowly, Harry, not too long now, not for too short a time, just right, so, then tip the burning mess from the dipper into the bowl of the pipe, inhale, mmmmm, once, deep, Harry, now again inhale, tipping your head back and dream.

Dream of those nights, one after another, eleven pipes one night, and chains of the sun, you said, like ice prepared to break into fragments, naked girls with peacocks under their arms, and panthers choking in blood. Red tins, he gave you, Harry, stuffed with your sticky dream machine, your smoking paradise. Tins that you emptied swiftly, night after night, on your own before the sun or with Caresse and your close friends, the couples you adopted. Dream back to those orgies with your sexual friends.

Four of you, five, maybe six, sharing a bed, sharing a pipe, sharing a way of life. Was that how it was? Were you ever jealous of the men touching Caresse? Were you, Harry? Or were you too absorbed yourself in their wives to worry about your own? Who was who in those endless opium nights when the cars flew through the darkened woods, and the bodies fell, screaming, or gasping, one after another, one on to another, one into another, clothed or clotheless, in shoes or out of them, in a dream of suns meeting and parting, the rush of leopards and fires, the hush of winds and waves, and the clicking of shutters. And the dogs. Floundering, furry and heavy across your copulations, tongue in cheek, or tongue in ear, or. Yes, Harry. I know the score. You wanted me to do it, sure you did, I remember the night after the black idol, and the dog coming with its thin stick scarlet as a lime twig, and the eager look in your eyes, and you pleading, urging, and I lifting my skirts and, I suppose I may have done, teasing the brute, and then feeling revolted and hauling back. And your anger, Harry. Recall how it was with everyone rolling and kissing and fingering here, there, and everywhere. A night of abandon. An orgy. An opium dream.

Dream, Harry. Dream that you're tired of being here, all alone, except for your paramour in annihilation, your sweet little Josephine, your dearly beloved former bed-mate and future companion in worm-feeding – dream that you want a walk, a break, a stroll out through the door again, and, yes, this time away from the blind alley of Mortimer's tiny studio, down a further flight of stairs, the emergency ones, or even out in the elevator, saluting the man working the doors with a nod and a cunning, conniving smile.

Dream your way out, Harry, and then dream your way back in. You can do it, you know. Take a look at your watch. Eleven minutes past six. Okay. So where will Caresse be now? And your mother? Still with your Uncle Jack, sitting there and waiting? Oh, I doubt it, Harry. They'll be back by now – worried, maybe, and not sure of what to do, but back, for sure – in their separate rooms at the Savoy Plaza, no more than a few quick blocks away. You could walk around – even take a run, keep you warm – be there in under fifteen minutes.

Remember the room. The view out across the East River, the long plunge down to the milling street, the dressing-table in the alcove. Imagine Caresse there, doing her hair. The brush with its bristles let into rubber stiff in her fingers, the tortoiseshell of the comb gleaming in dim light. Her dress off, on the bed. Her skin powdery, underthings that rustle along her thighs and her arms.

Remember, Harry. This was the night you were going with Hart to see the new Leslie Howard comedy, *Berkeley Square*. Strange. A play about a man who comes back from the dead to see the future. Just like you, Harry. It could be. You see, it has to be back from the dead, you know it has. The dead up here in this room, your Josephine. The dead who will follow after, yourself. Either very soon, by the gun, Harry. Or later, via the electric chair. There's no other way.

But, yes, you could still go. Walk down those twisting stairs – better give the elevator a miss, after all – and draw your collar up against the wind, and hail a taxi – no, again, better walk – and do the few blocks to the theatre at a fast pace, and go in, and stand, maybe just stand for a while, at the back of the stalls, and see Hart there by Caresse, his bullet head, and his bored look, and his eyes cruising for men in the wings, and her gaze, worried, abstracted, up on the stage, and your mother, worried, too, only more serene, expecting the best, even now, believing there must be some simple, proper explanation for the absence of her son, Harry Crosby.

Now it's twelve after six. Okay. So forget the theatre. They may not go, you know. They may worry too much to think of distracting themselves. You could stroll around and wait there in the foyer of the Savoy Plaza, maybe. Watch for the elevators coming down. The women in furs and high heels tripping out with their handbags and their thin umbrellas to meet their escorts. The men in the lobby smoking, reading the evening papers, pretending not to be irritated, stubbing their toes on the carpet, eager to get away.

Dream yourself there, Harry. Dream that you see Caresse, one last sighting, I guess, as she steps forward in mink and make-up, very much the suitable partner, for once, for your *soignée* mother, Harry, so beautiful, sure, so very beautiful she is. Brings tears to your eyes, I guess. Well keep those tears to yourself, Harry, I don't think after all you're going to get a chance to be shedding them out in public for all to see what a sad and sadly repentant sinner of a nice husband you really are.

No, sir. You'd better shed your tears into your black handkerchief rather quietly here in this room, with no one to see or hear except for your Josephine, Harry, your partner in death, your accomplice in party games. The only woman who saw your desire and acted upon it: me, Josephine. It's the way it is. It would be too great a risk to go out in the street, Harry. Too many chances of meeting a policeman and being spotted and having to come back up and have everything found the way it is now, before you've a chance to pull the trigger again and complete the picture. The mutual suicide. No murder. Just an agreement to die. But how many people will wonder whether you were murdered by me, Harry? How many people will think that I may have pulled the trigger myself and set the fuse burning that nothing, now, can ever put out?

Not many, I guess. I'm a poor weak woman. After all, Harry, a poor weak woman.

Seventeen

Last year, Harry. My year. Your year of gold when you struck the heart of the sun. Remember, Harry. The night before Bokhara. The evening you were still a man in love only with women.

Carried away, that's what you were, kidnapped in midstream by the riches of Boston – your mother, you told me, had made an unusual profit from Continental Can shares. She invited you both to go out from Paris and down to Milan and on to Brundisium, and across to Cairo, and share a long winter holiday with her in Egypt, the ancient sun kingdom, the land of Ra – and so you were taken forcibly, as it were, made to enjoy the freedom of Heliopolis under the iron hand of American capitalism. An odd affair, Harry. Very odd indeed.

The family trio. Another three–cornered structure this time, two women – mother and wife – and the common man, the uncommon subordinated man they shared. I mean you, Harry, pressed into plus-fours, or so it appears in that photograph you showed me, enscarved at the neck to keep you from cold, little boy lost, little boy crushed, is shown ensandwiched on the slopes of a crumbling phallic pillar at Baalbek, between two befurred and menacing, governing ladies, Caresse and Ma.

So how did the journey go? How was the long two-month

enslavement with moral arbiters at your side, and in your bed, and in the room next door not so very far away along the hotel corridor? How was the sense of pressure sustained and held at bay, and made sense of, Harry? How did you reconcile your enormous enjoyment of being abroad – at last, it seemed, at the sun's mercy – how did you fit this in with the green raincoat of the almighty dollar backing your sunburned spine?

I'll tell you how, Harry. You knelt one night, in black, atrocious darkness, on a small red mat, in a hired felucca on the Nile, and a Hindy tattooed the sun on your back, with only a swinging lantern to show him the place, and the blue needles ripping the flesh like the rods of a monk chastising himself, and your mother on shore, sleeping in fine linen with no dreams, and your wife, although there, forced to remain clothed, and have no tattoos herself, not even, as you might have well wished, Harry (I know your delicious tastes), a little wicked snake on the pink vulnerable architrave of her shaken penance, her vulva.

Tell me about the boy from the Temple you met and made love with – I know you did, Harry, your journals are thick with his praise. Were you waiting for someone like this all through those days in the eye-catching, scrofulous, flea-ridden streets of the Arab villages? Were you desperate for someone new, pent up night after night with only Caresse's familiar groin to enslave your tireless member?

You were, Harry. I know you were. Why, you even – you told me once in a black idol jag – you even felt lust spurt when you saw a gazelle flick its long eyelashes at you in the zoo in Budapest, and you sat afterwards through a fashion show in the foyer of the Ritz with your mind only on the tiny black and gold triangles under the underwear the girls were modelling, warming their shoulders in between under huge furs. Women in underwear and furs. It made you want your gazelle, your temple boy, your wife, even, again – what else was there still, Harry, to keep you calm?

You stood in the ruins of Baalbek in mid-winter, the sky

110

flecked with snow, the great legs of the columns crisped with a virgin white, and you threw five snowballs at the sun for the loves of your life, and a little one for Bokhara. Bokhara, the boy who had come – he said – rolled up in a rug from Bokhara to Jerusalem, and who threw down ink bombs from the four-star hotel on the passers-by with exactly the same abandon and pleasure you did yourself. Bokhara, Harry. Your lost youth, perhaps. Your onanism with your own boyish image.

Did you see his bared, sweating buttocks writhe, Harry? – I'm being indecent, I know I am, but so were you – when you paid a Turkish guide to take you to a club in Constantinople called the Turquoise, and then to a brothel, freezing cold, where you watched – and Caresse, alas, was there, too – a pair of stark naked heterosexual lovers engaged in a stylised, if at times aptly frantic, and well staged, and arousing coition? I'll bet you did, Harry. See little Bokhara nude there. And the big bronze actor cuckolding your own rights on the woman's translated and hopelessly quivering bottom.

So tell me, Harry. Tell me about the black Sudanese on the boat you saw sit rubbing his gleaming teeth for an hour with a stick as long as a phallus, a stripped stick as long as a man's erect member you called it. Was that in your mind, seeing him scrub his tusks, taking care, and using his time, was it how you would want to be using his flattened rear, which he kept out of sight on a rug on the deck, squatting cross-legged? Was it that you were really thinking about when you bargained and offered to buy the stick, and were sent away, and rejected, the man believing his tool to be worth far more than whatever you offered, your own toothbrush and a tin of tobacco and four silver coins?

I wonder. What was it that led you – lamb to the slaughter, it may have been – to the lizard eyes and the long yellow handkerchief waving of Champagne Charlie, who gave you a piece of hashish to eat? You ate it in one go, – 'as big as a caramel,' – you said it was, Harry – and after supper you felt all queer and went out to the Temple of Karnak and lay shivering under the moon afraid of fainting and feeling as if you were dying. And came back, and were in the hotel at Luxor with Caresse, and the following morning you felt worse – throat parched, giddy, depressed, resenting organ-isation – and even Champagne Charlie was astounded to hear you had eaten the lot at once. And you swore never again, and went on a donkeyback to the Tombs of the Kings, and there for the first time on your journey sensed an echo of the war, an echo to recur when you stumbled on wooden steps down to the underarm-smelling dugout they call the Tomb of Tutankhamun.

What was it, Harry? Was it the sense of Caresse ending, the long years with her growing stale in the constant compan-ionship? Was it the unavoidable closeness in two months of such isolating travel abroad, away from your books and your bars, your other friends, your quick pick-ups and your subtle deceits, or opportunities for them? Was it, Harry? Or simply that awful after-resonance of the war, more terrible than before, the undertow of the wing of death raking your bowels, like the time you hired a Ford and set out across the desert – the waste land, as it was – and you suddenly remembered the road to Bras and the utter desolation of the rows of wounded hopeless men in the mud and the flat unending treelessness of the shell-struck fields.

Whatever it was, Harry, it came to a high pitch, crested, and broke like the ninth wave of horror it was when you reached Constantinople, after the night in the brothel, after the couple screwing in frozen silence. And when you fell in with a man from the embassy whose birthday it was, and had more hashish with him, then opium pills, and champagne, and then hashish again to conclude the evening, the follow-ing day you were nearer to dying than any time excepting the day when the shell exploded your ambulance. Back there, you were filled with cataracts of gold, and with colours bursting. Later, there were flags flying on the embassy car your cousin loaned you to ride to the station. There were telegraph poles anad women burning at the stake and the wheels going clickety-click over firecrackers. Then finally, suddenly, there was something that touched a match to some hidden tinder inside your brain and your head cracked open and you exploded, exploded you said, right into the sun.

Whatever it was, it had happened again.

Eighteen

Orgies, Harry. Naked men wrestling – one painted silver, the other purple – for the favour of a Khmer girl's body. Girls making love to girls, the brown skin to the snake's forked tongue. Under the hot sun or at the Four Arts Ball. Were these your periodic release from writing? A brief, uneasy freedom from sitting down hour after hour, a holiday from the rough headstrong paragraphs of your diary, itself a controlled re-enactment of all the orgies and the nightlong parties? When did they begin to turn sour? Shortly before you came to Venice and the beginning of what would lead to this hotel room?

You charmed your way into the Four Arts Ball one year when Caresse was away. You were very drunk, and returned in a taxi, stark naked, your head spinning from the futile splendid reckless abandon of being with students and whores, doing exactly what someone, anyone, really, might please, and with anyone too, year after year, Harry, until that last year of 1928 when it all seemed suddenly boring and the climax was dry mouths and a dry sense of the party grinding in sand, like the keel of a pleasure steamer at its final, rather depressing destination.

The next year you talked Caresse into going too, trumpets and tom-toms, and the theme of the clothes was the French Revolution, and you both flirted or worse with Marat in red ochre, with Robespierre in a scum-bag with severed heads of the slumming virgins driven in like cattle to be divided amongst the rampant, the steers. It was hardly a success. You came home in an inner darkness, exhausted and still frustrated, spending the following day in bed with erotic books, your eyes and your brain teeming with what you had wanted, and failed still, to accomplish, the total surrender to the body's imperious demands.

Another time you fed a female monkey three gin fizzes – and for what, I ask myself, Harry, to open what orifice or desire in the furry creature, to let what energy of atrocious licence run free? There was a Russian princess you had your eye on, and then you were home again, drunk, and with nothing settled, except the need, no doubt mutual by now, for a certain sharing of aims, an oblique attack on the problem of how to squeeze the most from this endlessly beckoning affair, this night of available screwing.

There were long discussions, no doubt. A plan to give up the parties, to go no more. A plan to be drawn closer, to develop veins as yet unopened in each other. A third plan. To go free. Together and yet apart. Au-pair and yet with others. The free love plan. Alas, Harry, for both of you, and this you loathed – for your sweet and sexy wife as well as for your dear, frustrated self.

Lord Lymington, Harry. Describe this first and most aristocratic of Caresse's inamorati. Gerard Vernon Wallop Lymington, as blue-blooded as the stiff-upper-lipped English can come. And can they come? I wonder, Harry. I wonder. Could you have asked Caresse, or do you simply recall waking up in the dark, your head spinning, a wealth of thighs alongside your own, and hearing a sort of low gruff bark that was not a dog's, and a girl's thin yell, and feeling a quivering start in the mattress, and knowing, slumping down once more in the well of sleep, that the future Ninth Earl of Portsmouth, your own age, and infatuated with all you stood for yourself, had established once and for all both his territorial rights in a certain fuzzy triangle of wet flesh, and his power undiminished by alcohol or opium, to oblige this trembling place with the heavy coulter of his noteworthy ploughing?

Well, Harry. You were always jealous. You never enjoyed – except on principle, and then, after all, what is principle in the thrust of emotion? – the ecstasy of your own in the arms of other people. No. You turned over, then and on many nights, no doubt of this, and ground your face in the pillow, remembering the barrage at Verdun, and the sense of death, and the terrible drop right down into nothingness, and the hell of knowing you had to bite on the bullet, and tell no one, and be as good a boy as you could, for your pains, and roll to the left, and screw, if you could, whoever had planted her white rectum against your belly there, and let this be the price and the prize, a pound of jumbled skin, groaning and slapped in your moment of angry, possessive joy.

You gave your own party, the first of many, for eighty students and their womenfolk in your flat, an enormous champagne punch, with whisky and gin and Cointreau, and your costume, to be an Inca, was only a loin cloth, and a necklace of three dead pigeons, and a decoration of red ochre. You had your special Four Arts girl, your skinny model Raymonde in her peignoir, and Caresse wore just a chemise in blue silk, and had Lord Lymington to spur her on, and she rode nearly naked in the mouth of the great snake the students made in the Salle Wagram, waving to the lustful crowd from its fiery jaws, and her nipples, rouged with green, won the prize for beauty, and you were delighted – oh, sure you were – and were out cold on a pillar when Raymonde in her thin bones and her sheath found you, and felt afraid, and you left as a couple, for her place or for yours, and there was a red blanket, and the reek of dead pigeons, or taken women, and then oblivion.

It went on. Washing off the paint next morning in a hot bath, and taking a cold one to revive, and then reading aloud from *Venus and Tannhäuser*, the illustrations held up as stimulation before Bacardi cocktails, and a lunch with your father, and later a trip to the ballet and a sighting of James Joyce, a patch over one eye, and the day ending in cat-calls, and wild applause, and music.

The following year your father – your father, for God's sakes – was there. The furniture laid back to the wall, decks, as it were, stripped for action, the Chinese porcelains locked up and the bookcases turned to the wall, and your father, painted green like the rest of you, doing God alone knows what with whomever he could, some little silvered whore from Montmartre speaking no English except I love you, or maybe simply watching, I don't know. Anyway, more and more students came, and the punch flowed like before, Mortimer's own mix, and you wore this year seven dead pigeons instead of three – could you do it so many times in a single night in those days, Harry? – and you bought a bag of live snakes, and you all marched in a hectic procession, out from the flat and through the astonished streets to the hall, where three thousand students were going mad, and you climbed a ladder and tipped the snakes out, spitting above the dancers, and there was a mad screaming, and a couple screwing split apart, writhed, and were stuck together again with a snake round their shoulders, and a fat serious girl took another snake and fed it milk at her breast, and you saw a man drink from the skull you stole from the Catacombs which he had stolen again now from your library, and there were searchlights and roses, and Raymonde was there in red, and this year Caresse won no prizes, and you all went home in the pouring hard rain, and it was cold.

Very cold. And somehow you seem to have woken sober, Harry, to see your father off at the Gare St Lazare, a farewell drink of gin from a silver flask, and a port first on the way to the station, arriving an hour early nevertheless, and, yes, you must have been very cold and sober. Harry. Whatever the reason. Lord Lymington. Or someone else.

And then the last year. Last year. When you woke to find six in your bed, and the dog, and strangers in the flat, and you all took hot baths *à deux*, and you were soaping the

117

breasts of a little forget-me-not – and the best thing of all, you told me, was painting the women's breasts before the party began, the brush tickling the wry nipple, the pouting skin full with green, the body holding still, the lips eager, the surge in the groin held back for later. Painting breasts. Yes. That was the best.

So you rose and walked across the Tuileries, clean from the bath, and had a lunch of grapefruit and caviar and several sherry cobblers with Polia Chentoff, who was painting you both, and whom Caresse already loathed, and from there you went home to the sun in the courtyard, to the sound of an unknown couple having each other still upstairs in the salon, and then you were throwing books in a suitcase and finding a taxi, and so to the Orient Express and the wheels going, and a long sleep.

And this, Harry, was nine days before we would meet on the Lido and lie together in boiling sand and in deep understanding, and nothing would ever, I truly believe, be the same again. Not for the world, Harry, nor for you and me. It had started.

The end of the orgies. The slow focus down again into one woman's imperturbable, absolute soul, Harry, the subtle exquisite rejection of multiple excellence, and of slavering parties, the swift acceptance of being at one with someone more sharp to your mirror-image than anyone else has ever been. Believe me, Harry. I know what I'm saying. I saw the way it was the first day we met.

So remember Venice, Harry. The train arriving in the dawn sun, and the red cherries you had for breakfast on cold silver ice, and the wheels crossing the water, a lane of sweet light on the long lagoon. The gondola drifting you down the Grand Canal to the Hotel de L'Europe, and a room with a terrace overlooking the roofs and the bay, and then cold baths – were you still half covered with war paint from the last of the orgies? – and iced orangeades the colour of the sun setting.

So much sun. So much heat. The girls walking over the

bridges in frail pyjamas, you say. One girl in particular. The girl of the blue pyjamas. And the search starting. The horn blowing for the hunt. And then aborted, Harry. One morning on the Lido. One morning when you met your Fire Princess, your own Josephine, your wild-cat, your sun-lady, Harry. And here she is.

Be careful, Harry. Here she is. With black bobbed hair. And she eats men like air.

Nineteen

'I want to know, Harry.' That's what I used to say, time after time, in the icy cold, our breathing frosting into little puff-balls like Persian cats in the New York air, our hands nipping red whenever we took our gloves off to roll a snowball, or link fingers. We used to walk, Oh, sure, we used to walk. From the first moment I saw you across the misty ground at the Yale game a few months ago – your wife there, too, the bitch, in her grey squirrel coat and her silly muff – yes, from that second, Harry, when our eyes met in a hundred thousand pairs of eyes and you smiled, only for a short second, smiled, and I lifted my hand and might have waved, instead of arranging my hair under my new feathered hat, and smiled too (though as if to my sister, as if at a piece of the play) – I wanted to be close to you. From then, Harry, until you were in my arms by the fire on the twenty-second storey of the Hotel Victoria, seeing the green light swinging on the Ritz, or in your brain, there was nothing else I wanted or thought about or had anywhere near the centre of what mattered to me except our being together, and soon, a close, uninterrupted union.

Walking out into the falling snow that first night in New York, my fresh clean body against your bones. That's what it was. The closeness, Harry. The true presence, after six months of letters and awkward telegrams, of a voice on a wire, a fire voice as you called me, and now a substance to it, a thickness of breast or belly, a ripe flowering of the quivering pistil, the little foxy tongue from my chilled lips.

They would meet, Harry. Meet and part. On the sofa or in the snow, the same. Together in eager silence, the feverish slow devouring of all time into quickening bliss. For me, at least. For me, Harry. And then draw back, and then talk again. Walking and talking. Still or walking. Staring into a bright window of rings, or a cantilever of green candles and fir branches across the plate glass of an open counter, falling or rising hand in hand on a swift escalator, watching the gaudy trappings of Christmas range and fail, sinking below the imperious needs of our own bodies, Harry, the wish to be fondling and holding, reaching for what was warm and white under layer on layer of dark tweed, or a scarf of wool, or a pressing band at the waist, or a tucked-in-sweater here, or a taut stocking there. Our things. Our precious and shareable things.

The big flakes fell on our upturned faces as we chewed a hot dog apiece from a stall in Canal Street, and we breathed heat on the beautiful crystals, destructive as only human beings in love can be, enjoying our sense of fun, Harry, and swapping stories, and you allowing me to ask you questions which would normally, answered truly, have made me jealous. Yes. Jealous as hell, Harry. But not then. Not, somehow, then. We were too close, too safe, for once, to care.

Well. We made love then, that night, on the hard hotel bunk, writhing in slow abandon, and rolling over and using the floor, and the hot space on the rug in front of the fire, and then climbing on the sofa, turning, back to back and then front to back as I took you against my rectum, Harry. I love the word, like I loved the thing, the hard slap of your meat as it grooved me where no one had ever touched me before, ramming your force of desire in a space too closed as yet (it hurt, but I loved the hurt), and I opened and closed, and opened again, urging you on, as the last explosion sheared through my guts, as it seemed, and we went to sleep.

Oh, Harry. That was a night. You woke to find the fire out, and I heard you rise and stoke it, and then come back and stoke my body again, this time from the front, your eyes open and hot as fire itself in my own open eyes. Lewdness. The decorum of Boston tossed out the window into the snow, and the decency of knickers torn into shreds. Ripped as in rape. Rolled up and wrenched through with a screech of silk that excited us both.

You see, you loved me. I knew you did in those desperate, exploitative exchanges. Our twin bodies each crying out for satisfaction. Ignoring the other's pleasure, and thus being used, and enjoying the using, and knowing the loved one was happy, beyond reason, in doing what normally would be thought out of court, and so not done. Well, I lay and let you do what you wanted. I learned, and ached, and then took what I needed too. In my own way, in my own time.

Fear, nothing. We love it, Harry. Whatever we say, whatever we feel. It moves like a sleek banana out of its skin, and I want to eat it, Harry. I learned that, too, those nights in New York, those long days out walking through Central Park in the frost and the falling flakes, halting behind a tree, back to the trunk, slithering down, and then having my face guided to what you had opened, like a box of private and very special chocolates, your buttoned flies. I took it all, Harry. All in my mouth. Or so it seemed, feeling the fullness, the strange sense of possessing, the power to hurt.

I took it all. Two days together and two nights at the Hotel Victoria. And the chambermaid who found us half naked across the covers, snoring drunk, who ran out screaming, and so led to the bill being served, and our early departure. Two days. And seven more, after telephoning Mortimer, and a ride across town through the snow thawing and then beginning again, to this very room, Harry, this ninth-floor paradise where we did so many things, and I learned so much, and where you are now, Harry, and only one year later, going to have to learn what I have learned, how to die.

'So tell me, Harry. Tell me,' I asked as we lay later, under the quilt, and watched the lights through the drawn curtains, and heard the city filter in like strong coffee, after the worst, the best of all we did. Tell me the way it was when you heard my voice on the telephone at your father's house in Beacon Street. What did you do? How did you feel, Harry? Tell me the truth. I need to know. Tell me the shape of the Hispano-Mauresque plate on the wall, the feel of the contours of the brass drawer handles in the secretaire the telephone stands on, the sense of sweat in your trouserband, the dryness under your tongue. How did it feel? Tell me, Harry. Did you realise that this time after all you had really done it? Really persuaded someone? That this was your destiny you were talking to?

Fire. Princess of Fire, that's what I was, Harry, that's what I am still, mistress of burning coal and of cold embers, the cinder queen, in the cold furnace now, alas, and for ever, Harry, but still the lady of flames, the place of heat and of comfort. Unlike the cold, ethereal image of your Grey Princess. Jacqueline. Oh, I know, Harry. Jacqueline never was. She was just an idea, an image. You tried to reassure me so many times, running your fingers through my hair after you'd woken once with her name on your lips, and I'd risen, frantic, and run out into the corridor at the Hotel Victoria, and you were frightened a maid would see me, or even, maybe, that I'd throw myself down the stairwell – and I tell you, Harry, I might have done, oh boy, I sure might, the way I was feeling then, the first time I heard her name.

You'd seen the lady of the Zorn etching – your Jacqueline – in 1924, and kicked yourself for not buying the girl with her legs apart and her stick between her knees, bare-foot, staring ahead, and exactly, yes, I think that was worst of all, Harry, exactly like you. No wonder Caresse hates that oil painting you told me about, the one where Polia Chentoff paints you with staring eyes, and you look more like your Jacqueline than anyone else. No wonder, Harry. No wonder I nearly threw myself down the stairs. It was me you looked most like, Harry. Before the etching came, it was me. It made me laugh till my heart almost broke with joy when you wrote to say that your jade lady had seen my photograph on your desk and had asked if that were your sister, we looked so alike, you and I, so much like two splinters thrown from the same slice of the axe – twin heads now on the block though, Harry, think of that.

Jacqueline. Josephine. So close. The same beginning and the same end, and only the middle for me to have something different from, to feel perfectly sure in the original sin with, the original love, to erect as my special castle of love, my personal syllable where no one else could ever enter and steal you away, my Harry house, my little inner shrine. Well. I still have that, Harry. I still have that.

You told me once – when I got better, when I could accept the idea of your love for a phantom – of how you booked a table for two at Chez Philippe in Paris, and had her out for a meal, and ate your way through the whole three courses ordered for both. The imaginary Jacqueline's empty chair facing you there across the gleaming steel and the napkins, and waiters as deferential as usual, used to such mad behaviour, serving food with their dextrous, normal skill, pouring the wine, even, you told me, and, yes, I almost believe you, asking once if mademoiselle would enjoy some mineral water after her wine, and then, as you rose, drawing back her chair, and bowing to see the two of you out.

She was dressed in grey. Grey like the sea on the beach at Manchester, grey like the winter sky above the Sun Tower, grey like the pelt of a silver fox or a mink. She had wide eyes, like yours, she had a serious sensual mouth. She had strong hands, and strong toes, and a belly wide enough to be carrying a child. And, yes. She has her place in your will, I'll bet, Harry, like that little rude Arab boy in Palestine, and how many more, they'll never find, God knows. And me, too. Maybe me, Harry. You never say. Good luck for Albert. Let him spend it, if they ever ratify – which, of course, they won't.

One winter day you woke and saw the snow spread out like a clean blanket over your land, and you wrote me the precious letter that never fades – the colours are now grey cramoisy fire gold star, fire being the centre – and I knew that the battle was won, Harry, and that we were one, as we had to be, and you knew it, and that everything was going to be all right, as I'd feared it might never be. Day after day, as they came, my letters had burned their hole in your brain, and you were a creature of fire now, like a little demon with a forked rod spry in the heart of hell.

Maybe it was black idol. Maybe it was the snow. Maybe it was just the others burning away, the way they had to. The star always paling before the crackling flames. The grey obliterated by the blaze. The scarlet seeming at last a part of this blaze, a harbinger of the full spectrum wrought in the flame. At any rate, you were mine, Harry. Mine, like a hearth of coal. Mine, like a branch chopped for burning. Mine, only mine.

You learned to write. You put all of yourself in your best poem, the one you wrote the day before you sent me that letter, the poem you sent me as 'Sunflower', the heartpiece of your *Mad Queen*, and the revelation of the terrible energy that we are, Harry, that we have to be together, the twin spirals of change, the obliterators, the fiery engines of a new world.

In the next two days you made it perfect. You gave it a context – your time in Istanbul when the sun exploded out of your brain, and you nearly died. How many times have you come so close to dying, Harry? The ambulance at Verdun in 1917; your party with a man from the embassy, in 1926; and, oh yes, a final clinching time – today, December 10th, 1929. There's always black idol, the rush and surge of the fire to your brain, or the flood of the kif, Harry, the hashish setting its ultimate seal on the other intake, the way it did that night with the Kurd shepherds, after the dancing, and the drive home through the darkness.

Hashish. And the hashish-eaters. The assassin, who work-ed up their blood for the killing of Christians, the way you

and I have to work up ours for the death of the simple
vulgarity of the world, Harry, the assassination of self in the
private eternal contemplation of the inner suns rising, twin
and special, ours for ever. So. Assassinate yourself, Harry.
The time will be soon. Get ready. The way I didn't need to
be ready. The way I keep myself ready, always. And make
the move. Pull the trigger. Fire the shot.

In time, though, Harry, in time. There's more to be
spoken. More to let thread through the air of this quiet room
like the cotton along a reel from some future sewing-mistress
of suicide to unravel. More to be taking out of your own
mouth, your own heart, and let slide through my own filter,
Harry. Speaking the truth. Saying the way it has to be.
Showing the way it was, or ought to have been.

Twenty

Tell me, Harry, why did you learn to fly?

I never flew, Harry, except with you. Time after time, through black idol, in bed, on the floor, on the sands of the Lido. You taught me to do what I wanted to do in the air. The aerodynamics of love, Harry. Aphrodite in Flight. It's too late now. Your poems will come out when we're both in the ground, not in the air. Two lost lovers who leave a manual for all future astronauts of the air. Two star-crossed lovers, Harry. In flight from the world of all that seems putrid and stale.

Lindbergh. It's a name to me, too, goddammit, Harry. You can't be alive in the 1920s and not know exactly the way that lean bronzed figure looked when he raised his face into the ticker-tapes, the whole of Broadway showering down its business confetti to celebrate the marriage of American genius and untamed air. Solo across the Atlantic. So much for the European achievement. Alcock and Brown. A pair of aviators. Two for company. Like a firm of country solicitors, as they call them in England. Where was the danger, where was the glamour in that?

It's eight o'clock. It's May 21st, 1927. A cold spring light, and no gin left in your flat when you reach the field. You, Harry. Caresse, huddling close for warmth. Your father. Grumpy, no doubt, and with his whistle. I wonder if he blew his whistle when *The Spirit of St Louis* landed. Like recognising a goal at football.

Oh, I know it all. The way it was. Like so many more nights racing from Paris to see a friend, or to drink the new wine at some farm, or to see the sea, or simply – sure, very often – to enjoy the wind in your hair and the sense of speed. Not this time, though. Crawling. Slow slow slow. In that long metal crocodile of adoring wheels, creeping down the Seine to Le Bourget, eight miles of frustrating agony from Paris, to see the landing.

We wanted our own hero. One hero. A solitary cowboy of the clouds, a gunslinger behind the twirling propeller. Lonely across the ocean. Someone we could all identify with. The guys could be. The girls could love. And he looked exactly like you, Harry. Lean, bronzed and blond. I guess you noticed that when the hush fell on the great crowd in the cold.

Nothing, though. Nothing at first. Only the fireworks building their flowers into the darkness, only the piercing scalpels of searchlights meeting and crossing. Probing and finding nothing. Just like the war, someone mutters. Laughter. Scraping of heels. Shivering.

Listen. A dull throbbing. Someone's coming. 'Heh, you guys, he's here. Lindbergh's coming. He's here.' But no. Only a French flier, doing acrobatics to please the crowd. Using up the last of the twilight in a frenzy of looping and then down, stowed away in a large hangar to a dulled ripple of applause. No one was wanting a circus that night. There was too much screwed-in emotion, too much intensity of feeling, for that.

Silence again. Shuffling of feet. Low voices. Then another throbbing. A loud roar. And the London Express came in, like a huge ray, settling, disgorging passengers, baggage, crew. Threading their way through the serried waiting faces, tired, less interested in Lindbergh than in Paris, home, a bath, bed. Then suddenly. Another more throaty sound out of the utter blackness, a swooping white shape, like a small white hawk, you said, and the flight was over. There he was, upright in the cockpit, slightly dazzled in the sudden flash of cameras, glow of searchlights, warmth of the adoration from all those excited eager faces. Here was their saviour, here was their man of the air.

Tell me, Harry. Tell me how it was. The trouble is that I'm dead, you see. I can only take you over. I'm not myself any more. I'm just a voice, the voice of the way it was. The voice of the radio or the newspapers or the secondhand impressions of ordinary inarticulate people who talked about it afterwards in their own words. I lie here like an amplifier, sending back whatever came in when I lived, whatever might have come in. It's magic, Harry. Nasty magic, when some-one's dead.

The body lies here like a piece of clay. It assumes whatever it wants to, or whatever its owner might have wanted it to, if its owner had lived. Sure, the body. That's what I am now, Harry, the way the police will see me. The former Josephine Rotch. The former Josephine Bigelow. A stretch of skin and bone about five feet eight inches long, with short hair, and some lovely clothes, and a string of pearls like drops of sweat, and a pair of silk stockings you could make a parachute from, and a crushed sponge in her skull you could squeeze all the news of Europe, all the misfortunes of history, all the wonder and genesis of your own terror out of, Harry. Sure. A sponge that was once a brain with its own pretty or terrifying or lustful or wonderful secret ideas breeding. Sure. A sponge, though. Able, and still able – I tell you, Harry, I know what I'm saying, it's me that's dead, not you, so far – able to soak up all that you want to give or put in.

So tell me now. What was it like? What was it like when the crowd started to move? When the hundred thousand faces began to turn as one towards the man in the cockpit, the God of the Air there in the cross from the sky, the lord of the flying machine? What was it like when they started to run? All together. Huddle, muddle. Pell mell. Stumbling. Shout-ing. Dropping things. Jostling each other. Urged as one being towards the tiny painted moth alighted there in a circle of French policemen at the heart of the field. Racing. Outdistancing each other. Falling. Muddying coats. Losing shoes and handbags. Crying out. Singing for joy. Screaming in pain. Knocking each other over. Reaching out their hands to handle, to touch, the wings of the little machine, like the hem of Christ's garment, anxious to be filled with the same virtue, the magic elixir, as had borne the aviator across the surging Atlantic, safe and sound. The defeater of death in the waves. The master of the air and the clouds.

What was it like? It was hands. Hands, you said. I remember, Harry. A hundred thousand pairs of hands. Like maggots. Everywhere on the aeroplane. Crawling. Devouring whatever there was to be eaten. Yes. That's what I remember. Take, eat. This is my body. Tear my flesh in the absence of any ritual. Strip me like locusts, clean to the bone.

Later that year, on Armistice Day, the students came in as the year before and you drank two jeroboams of champagne, remembering the war and the black and silver pilot who took you up in his little biplane above the firing line. Two jeroboams of champagne and later two glasses of brandy, alone at night, smoking, and remembering your token dead, Oliver Ames Junior and Aaron Davis Weld. They had to stand for so many.

Later still, you remembered the shell that shattered your ambulance, and the white light rising into a sea of dust, and the face of God resting there like Apollo's, dark as the muzzle of an Egyptian hound, and you dipped the paw of Narcisse Noir into black ink and signed his name. For whosoever calleth upon the name of the Lord shall be saved. 741. Mashed into pieces. Nothing remaining. Seven and four is eleven and one is twelve. Two and one is three. Caresse and yourself and another. A woman, Josephine. A dog, Narcisse Noir.

Remember, Harry. Always remember. You saw the face of your own death in the flash of a shell exploding, the disintegration of a vehicle. So remember. What was it like for

Lindbergh alone out there a few skimming feet above the waves, the churning blackness, the lethal Atlantic with all its rays and its whales, its disintegrating wrecks, its keels of so many ships from the days of the Norsemen to the icy night that sent the *Titanic* to rest amidst the sands? What was shifting there inside his concentrating or nodding brain as he swept the dark waters, Harry? Did he see his own death coming sometimes, did he feel the cold hand on his sleeve in the blue cockpit, the bony fingers of what would send him down in a nose dive to the far bottom, the irrecoverable place where nothing lives except the dreams and the flattened fish with no eyes that creep in solitude?

What was it like to be alone? To be so alone there was no human sound except the roar of the airscrew, no human sight except the yellow dials as they indicated the petrol running out, no human memory except of a lost forgotten field in a country they used to call America where his wife and his child were waiting, hoping he might return. Was it like the war? Was it like the isolating darkness around those fragile ambulances, plying night after night away to the Front and back, no one there except the dead and the dying, the few with enough blood to keep them going to the dressing station, the many without any change in their veins or their pockets and only the blackness to look forward to, the cessation of pain?

What was it like to guess at pain, to imagine the sudden stop of the engine, the drop of the safe, encircling wings, the plunge into coldness, and then down, down, further than any dive in a pool or the bleak sea at Coffin's Beach, or anywhere else along the Atlantic Coast, further than life itself, further even than hope, feeling suddenly the skin of your skull cracking open, the way yours cracked open, Harry, like the yolk of an egg coming out in a frying pan, and the pure white catching fire, drowning, sinking for ever into nothingness, a box padded with velvet the size of a continent.

Was he able to live through, in those lone hours, what you lived through in that fresh second? The years of irredeemable

131

loss, the sense of failure, the moods of a lifetime cancelled into one mood, the heartrending knowledge of going out like a light – or was he there like a footman, an undertaker in the wings of his own death, Harry?

This you believed, Harry. Seeing your own face in his when he stepped from the cockpit into the cheering crowds. This you believed. Remembering other flyers, other flights. Always the sense of isolation, the sense of speed. The great wings rising, towards the sun, away from darkness, and through the darkness. Under control. The control of the pilot's hands, the true hands, the single pair of hands familiar with all the disembodied machine could do, able to touch it with pride, and reverence.

I can feel the flutter already of all that rush of ticker-tape. I can hear the roar of the traffic stopping on Broadway. I can see the faces, a million New York faces, looking down, as we look up (out of our graves, Harry, out of our coffins) into their wondering exhilaration, throwing their town lives down, the diaries of all they worried about, knowing that we've chosen a way to stop the decay, to be pure and lucid for ever, the true winners, the pair who crossed the Atlantic alone in each other's arms, as brave as Lindbergh. Remember, Harry. That's how it's going to be.

Twenty-One

I know why you learned to fly two years later, Harry. I
know. It's there already in black and white in your diary.
Another reason, less romantic for sure. You were jealous of
an aviator called Meier who was wounded in the war. The
Aviator. Cord Meier. Tall and alert in his light leather flying
jacket, skin bronzed a little, the same as yours. Hair light,
eyes keen and shrewd. Limping, maybe. A war hero. A
flyer. No wonder, Harry, he made his mark. No wonder he
caught the eye of Caresse, eager the way she was to make
you jealous now, knowing my fire letter was burning its hole
day after day through the cloth of your trouser pocket, sure
that the one thing you would find it hardest of all to accept
was her going out with a war hero, a man very nearly the
same – in background, in his carefree spirit, in all that he felt
about wild adventures and new experience – sure, very
nearly the same as you were, Harry. Very nearly. Only,
maybe, even more so.

Watching them drinking sherry cobblers, walking through
the trees into the wood by the stream, talking and laughing,
Caresse putting her arm through his, you began to fall back
in love with her, to desire her again, or to think you did, and
to hate her, too, Harry, the way you hate every woman you
fear may be going to leave you. I know just how it felt when
you sulked all day upstairs in your study, and studied the

photograph you used to have in your wallet of Caresse nude, and played the phonograph, over and over, a melancholy tune. I know it well, I played it myself night after night thinking of the needle turning not in the record but in Caresse's stretched white skin. It's a sad tune, Harry, an evaporator of rage, and it helps, not to forget, but to live with the jealousy you cannot ignore. I too have known despair, Harry, and the need to cling.

No wonder it fascinated your wife, to see someone do all those aerial dances across the great scoured floor of the clouds, and to come down alive, and be ready for more tomorrow, after, no doubt of this, a reviving night of love in the interim, and with someone new and already spoken for, a wife of a poet, a sort of failed aviator of the ground, a wordy man of wings, clogged in his own propeller, unable to lift off and soar.

No wonder. No. So you made your decision, Harry, and entered your name, and put down your four hundred dollars, and in no time you were up in the air, and then down on the ground for a long session with your instructor, Detré, to perfect your sense of the many controls.

You were nervous, though. You cut your great library down, vowing to reduce the books to a basic one thousand, breaking your glasses, and again breaking another pair, as you fumbled with useless pages, pained with toothache and reading Proust, and releasing carrier pigeons, and watching them go, and only some return.

You were taking passifloreine to calm you now, and you laid the most money you ever laid on a horse, and you read in the evening newspaper that the World's Speed Record had been shattered by a Schneider Cup flier at three hundred and sixty miles an hour, and this very day you sat down and synthesised what you felt about the Aviator and Caresse in a sequence of poems you called *Aphrodite in Flight*.

The mania fades, Harry. It always fades. You woke up with a bad head, and had three more spoonfuls of passifloreine, and Alaska cocktails, and then yellow Chartreuse, and the news came through on the ticker-tape that the horse that had won the St Leger was Trigo, with second Bosworth, and then Horus third, and Hotweed nowhere, and this brought your losses for the year thus far up to two thousand five hundred dollars, and still, Harry, still, the poems lie in their folder there, unpublished, maybe they never will be.

You flew every day, sometimes twice, learning to bank, learning to do turns, learning – or hoping to learn – to fly cross country the way you used to run, and watching, always, Detré, doing acrobatics in between instructing, and then one day – did it seem an omen, Harry? – you shot a pheasant, and poured a magnum of champagne over your hair to celebrate. And the Aviator was back, and with Caresse. She went to Paris, and the distance between you could grow some nights to the breadth of the Russian steppe he had flown across, as barren as that, and as icy, too.

The worst, perhaps, was when she bought you a book, *The Art of Flying*. Oh, sure. A perceptive gift. After your own poems, though, on the aerodynamics of love, it struck home like a clear indication of what was wrong. Think on the ground first. Before trying anything in the air the pilot should devote thought to it on the ground. You knew what she meant, Harry. She was always a slow starter. She needed foreplay. You were too fast off the pad for her.

Reaching, then, for the core of the matter, the place of origin, the heart of the flower, knowing that sometimes it hurt to be hurt, Harry, the way it was with me, the reason it may be we do so well together, flying duo, understanding the way to be up in the air fast, as in a vertical take-off machine, a magic swooper – yes, you tried to be more the way she wanted, and to make her, too, be more the way you wanted, and neither worked, and the Aviator still came, and went satisfied, as did Caresse, and the year languished, and you grew daily more sure of yourself at the stiff controls.

Sure of yourself. Reading my fire letters, and waiting. Yes. 'Let the pilot visualise difficult situations in flight and think out the correct way to recover from them.' You became better at that, flying in rain, tossed about like a tennis ball in a tempest, in equinoctial storms, dreaming of aeroplanes, and of orchids, dreaming of women, dreaming some fifteen-year-old girl you saw at the races was there in bed with you, and then waking to fly again. Buttoning on your leather helmet, easing the flying suit on your arms, eager to be flying solo, cursing the weather that held you back, flying in wind and held back from flying in fog.

Finally, Harry. Flying six times in a single day, four times in the morning, two in the afternoon, and knowing that the solo flight must at last be the following day. As it was. On November 11th, Armistice Day, you made your flight at the famous eleventh hour, holding the two wings aligned, as you knew now how to do, in the blaze of the sun.

Landing, how was it? How did it seem, when you unbuttoned the flap of your helmet, and felt the earth again underfoot, and knew that you, too, were now an Aviator? How did it feel? I know how it felt, Harry. It felt the same. And your plea that you have no funeral, that you want to be burned, and your ashes taken up in an aeroplane at sunrise and scattered into the wind, and that you be purified in fire, and float free over New York City – why, Harry, it may, after all, soon come to pass.

But the Aviator will still be alive. And so will Caresse.

Twenty-Two

This summer, while you were discovering that flying alone cured nothing, Harry, I was married. Jacqueline wasn't my only rival even then, I knew there was one more. I know now who it was. I found out one day not so long ago when you showed me a few sheafs of your diary. You chose with care from your file, and I saw your face move, and I waited until you were in the bathroom before opening the folder and taking the rest out. You came back angry. I was already reading the letter A, and the word sorcery, and you snatched the file and said, 'You mustn't look, I haven't finished those, I've told you before,' and I schooled my looks and said, 'I'm sorry, Harry,' and that was all, it was quickly forgotten.

Forgotten by you, Harry. But not by me. I took my time and I waited until you were fast asleep, and I shifted the covers, and stepped out on the board floor, and found your suitcase. The locks were open, and there was the whole diary, for me to read, and I read it all, Harry, the finished, and the unfinished, the rough and the smooth, the bits about me and the bits about Caresse, and, yes, the entries about the Sorceress.

The Sorceress. The cat-witch. The Queen of Egypt. My rival for the columns of print that would make us famous, accepted or feared by the Boston hierarchy, the bloods and the outcasts. She was married within a couple of months of my own engagement. Wife of a classics scholar, a coming professor, a man who will one day, I guess, be a pillar of the old régime, and bring honour and a fresh patina of the ancient forms to our aching, tottering Boston.

Sure he will. But not her, Harry. She was a wild-cat. A puma, you called her. A panther, sometimes. A great black streak of sex and energy, and a flair for clothes, and a taste in jewels, a gift for making her body seem all electric current, and urgent for switching on. She was ready, evidently, and came commended by Archibald MacLeish (God rot him), who thought she might be amusing to you and your wife.

Amusing. Well. You saw her as pure physique from the very first, drinking cocktails from half past five, and knowing already you meant to have her, and not for talking to – oh no, for the whole thing, Harry, the full plunge you were getting still, but with less affection, and less power, and less lust, and less abandon, from sweet little ageing Caresse, used up overnight on her English lord, and her Spanish gypsy a time or two, and her, most of all, her coming Aviator. Coming, yes. It was what she saw in your eyes that first night.

Holding hands, and some sharing of mutual jokes, and a walk or two in the woods, with the vigilant scholar always at hand, and a raft of royalty on the donkeys, and always, too, the sun shining, and the heat feeling for your parts under the plus-fours and the striped sweater, and under her black dress, and her necklaces, and her slippers. Already, yes. Those red slippers that sent you wild.

So Caresse took what she could, and there were quarrels, and she left on a holiday. I was married then. In Santa Barbara, on my honeymoon, and it was clear enough what was going to happen. Poor Albert. He wasn't any better – he isn't any better – than I had supposed he would be. You see I'd been virginal with Albert, the way I never was with you. He wanted it that way.

So there we all were. The Sorceress already worn out and tired with her active and always present scholar, and ready for something new, and you, Harry, no doubt with me on your mind, or me blocked out of your mind, or me about to be writing to you, and you waiting for me. And me slinking along the beaches in California, in that strange American sun, and sunbathing, smooching with casual beaux at beach dances, and making Albert feel cuckolded already, and letting my body be taken at night under the thin sheet, and holding stiff, and enjoying it very little, neither the taut squiggle, nor the penetration, nor the aftermath of blind kisses.

There we were. Caresse abandoned, or feeling so, and Albert never accepted, and the strong scholar not knowing what was soon going to hit him. The losing ones. The figures in the backdrop. And the leading players? You and I, Harry. Stoking up for the final fire. And the Sorceress, the witch, intervening, a red-hot poker to pitch you into a different furnace, but only for a week or two, Harry, only until I had had my fill of pretending to be Mrs Bigelow, and decided to write, and lower my grappling irons into the ocean again, and catch your available body into my arms.

You had her, Harry. Of course, you had her. On an evening with gin fizzes, green and silver, and finding her just the same as you had expected. You saw her again, at the Ritz, and you walked on to your lawyer's, and wrote out what you called a new testament.

So many thousand here, so many there. And I'll bet I know whose name came in for the first time, Harry, and why you went the same day as you saw her. You couldn't leave things alone, could you. It always had to be a matter of bequeathing what you possessed, seeing the future of death, and the people surviving, the rings and cups left over, the gold renewed in the living hands, and the girls who were fresh and alive given what they deserved for their services to your body. Girls, and, of course, your one boy, the little catamite, Bokhara.

So all will be rewarded. Or, rather, they won't, Harry. Not after you've pulled the trigger and become a suicide, or a killer, or both, and your will gets read over, and the coroner or the judge or whatever decides you were mad, Harry, and that the will be null and void, therefore, and the money all go to Caresse, and the gold, too, and the manuscripts, and the foul diary. Foul, I say, Harry, for that ugly Sorceress in it. Her gross breasts, and her stinking thighs, and her great wet lips globbering over yours.

Well. You got my letter. It must have carried advance force like a coming gale, you were warned I suppose, because you began to consider its possibility again in your speculating print before it arrived. And it did arrive. On August 27th. Pure gold, as you say. Pure fire. I remember sitting up late in the dressing room at the new house in Warrender Square, a Boston bride with a snoring husband, all alone in my blue gown and my white suspender belt, and I wanted you Harry, I wanted you very much, and I knew that the time had come to choose.

Choose, no. I had always chosen. The time had simply come to declare the choice, and to put the clear message into words, digging my pen deep into the cream-laid vellum-style correspondence paper. My hand shaking, the smell of powder filling the air, the sound of a snoring filtering through from the other room, where I would shortly bequeath my body, Harry, knowing he might not even wake, even feeling my sweet hand on his penis, between his thighs. Knowing I wouldn't care if he did, and woke, and grunted, and rolled over, and took me face down on my belly, gripping the pillow not to scream, but not with desire, Harry, with loathing now, with a pure revulsion, and wanting only you, wanting your clean hair, and your ice eyes, and your great thing thick and strong in my mouth.

I wrote all this. I know. Shameless, and hating Boston. Hoping, almost, that Albert would wake, and walk in, and find me writing these lewd, impossible words. To someone else. Knowing me yours. All of me. Body and soul to use. The way you wanted to use me in life or death, Harry. The only way I could have you – I knew that then as I know it now – the only way I could make you most absolutely and for ever and ever mine.

So I sealed the envelope, and I put it into my bag, and the following day I mailed it express rate to Mortimer in Paris. I knew you would have it very soon, and would know that the marriage was nothing, and we were a couple, a pair of united lovers the way that we'd been in New York City.

I knew that I had you then.

Had you, yes. Despite the return of the Sorceress in October, all big hips in elastic, sweet as the falling chestnuts, no doubt, the day she came back and you smoked a black cigarette with her, and there again was her mouth, and her swaying, tight dress, and her slippers.

A cold, grey day. At least for me. But it couldn't last, Harry. I knew it couldn't. You meant to come back to New York, and to live on the Ritz Tower with someone, and, sure, it was going to be, whether you knew it or not, Harry, with me. For a few weeks more you had cigarettes, and the tight dress, and the red slippers. Then me.

Slippers, though. Why those? You always wanted me in high heels, Harry. Tottering towards you like something out of the Moulin Rouge, with my cheeks painted, and a man's cane in my hand, and my stockings drawn up as high as I could, silk and sheer, and the shoes, black, streamlined like racing cars, and with thin tall heels. Like that. One night, anyway, when we found the cane and a top-hat, and some white scarves that Mortimer had in a press, and you made me dress up, Harry, be someone out of a play for you, a sex-mad schoolgirl for a time, and then someone playing a man in a cabaret.

You came, then. On November 16th. You took the *Mauretania* for New York City, with Caresse and Constance, and every day of that long familiar voyage there was one of your girls to think about. On the 17th you had her telegram, the witch's telegram, saying simply 'YES'. Yes. I wonder, Harry. Yes to what? Yes to your love, or yes for her own love, or yes – was she really up to this, to what I was giving

141

you yes to, Harry – to dying with you?

The following day you were playing baccarat with the Lady of the Golden Horse, tiny jade hands, golden like false netsuke, on the triangles of the board. And on the 21st, with Caresse in the cabin asleep, you wrote out for her a fair copy of what you had written for her, but planned, I know, for me – your dreams of love, the poems you called *Sleeping Together*.

But already you had my last fire letter in your pocket, a wall of flame, a terrible blaze of light through the tweed of your suit, and you must have walked the decks red as coal, a man of embers and tiring heat, nothing left of you except the cinders waiting for me to be breathing them back into high flame. Oh, Harry. The rest were nowhere now. You were coming to me. You were mine. I was yours. There was nothing left in the whole world except the wind and the great ship shaking, and you there with your hair blowing in the wind, and me in your pocket, Harry. Me. Josephine.

Twenty-Three

The tape reels in my head, and I hear you telling me what to say, to put the record straight, to see that the future will know exactly what led us both up to what has to happen, finally and irrevocably, in just a few minutes. The second shot. The clincher, Harry. Let the words come out of the air and into my brain, like a spiral of smoke, an Indian signal, a sword for my throat to swallow, or rather a flame, then spout forth and up, words like a salamander or phoenix. The truth. The real thing. The way it was.

All that time apart, and then together again. That's how it seemed, Harry. That's how it was. Nearly a year, and a child, and a marriage, away, a lifetime of being alone and waiting for you, keeping the sense of liaison alive on the frail thread of a letter or two, waking each morning alongside the wrong body, hearing the wrong voice talking in sleep, or snoring, or calling my name every night through the door, from the hall. It was hard.

And then, suddenly, you were there. I put on my best dress, the one with the sequins in gold, and the plunged neckline fanning out like the veins of the sun, and I touched my ears with a faint scent of Nuit d'Or, and I walked in my thin dark mink through the wind and the nipping air to the public library, and for half an hour – I was early, Harry, I had to be there in time – I leafed through boring book after book in the engineering section, the natural history section, the curved series of shelves with volumes on politics and on social science.

Nobody cared. Nobody noticed my hands trembling, the way my eyes flicked up every time a man came by, the slight uneasy movements my lips made when I tried to read, or pretend to read. I was just another outcast among so many, seeking a warm room in the heart of winter, a place to store up a little energy for the battle home out of the cold, a girl with a need to learn, to improve her mind, to get on in the world.

Nobody either of us knew in Boston ever read a book, Harry. No, for sure. So it was the ideal place to arrange a meeting. I told you that when I wrote, when I gave the pompous old butler my letter for you at the door in Beacon Street, and muffled my face in my fur, and walked quickly away, and never looked round, and never knew if he knew who I was, or what I looked like, and hardly cared.

I was much too excited then to care. It was different later. Boston was in my blood, Harry, a little, just a little. I couldn't slough off the need to be discreet so easily. So I chose the public library, where the down and outs gathered, a haven for the respectable outlaws, of either sex, who didn't drink, or talk aloud, or do things to themselves with their hands, but who lacked a purpose, and found some sense of one amongst the books, the words of the dead, and the great newspapers.

Then you came. I felt your hand on my shoulder, under my fur, and I looked up, and you were smiling, Harry, all blue eyes and fair hair, and a black gardenia, and the rays of the sun, so it seemed, streaming out of your neck and up to the fumed-oak walls like a blaze of light. You smiled. And I guess I smiled, too, and I don't know what I said, or where we went, except that we held hands, deadly daring, out in the street, and then there was gin, and I was burning, and wanted you there and then, in the bar, and reached for your hand, and put it right up on top of my stockings, and felt the fingers uncurl like the fronds of a fern, and stroke the keyhole between by thighs.

Pamela, Harry. I feel her turning again. She moves inside me, the way you moved inside me one hour later that day, when we found a way to be just the two of us at Robert's flat. She remembers. She felt her father that morning, hot as the ball of the great sun across her cradle behind my skin. She knew who you were, Harry. She turned then, as she turns now, and I cried out, I remember crying out, the way the child herself seemed to cry, when you reached as far in as you could, and the tide of generation rushed white and wild once again in my frightened body.

Afterwards, tea. And a walk through the frozen trees back through the park, and our plans made for the next few days. You would see the Yale game with Caresse, then she would go on to New York City, and you would stay with your parents in Boston. Albert would go to my mother's on Commonwealth Avenue, to work. And Robert, sweet Robert, your sister's former husband, eager, it seemed, to promote yet another family schism, would lend us his house. Lend us, and stay away.

For five days we were alone together. Or almost. Under the hinge of Boston, staying indoors, mostly, with the curtains drawn, and the bottles of gin mounting up on the floor, and the phonograph always being cranked up on the little Sheraton table, and Robert, occasionally, but ever so ever so discreetly, knocking to ask if we knew the time.

Then came Thanksgiving. Thanksgiving for what? It prised us apart. You ate at home with the family, and then took the train to Caresse in New York. For four days I tormented myself, alone. I ground my nails in my palms, I tried to read all the letters you ever sent me, I walked up and down the same street, I went out with Robert, I felt the tears breaking through my eyes whenever I saw a man with fair hair. It smashed me, Harry. I couldn't last.

On the telephone, crouching over the black receiver, whispering so that the servants wouldn't hear, at the wrong hour, in the wrong clothes, shivering in the draughty hall, wondering if Albert might, after all, come back for a book or a brief, I told you how I felt, knowing you couldn't, or wouldn't, be quite yourself, with Caresse no doubt over your shoulder, or worse, in your arms, but making you understand, in the simplest words, that I had to see you, I had to come to New York.

Well, Harry. You moved fast. You saw how it was and we went to Detroit. I reached you at the Hotel des Artistes, and we went on from there. At once, to the train. I stubborn, you furious. Neither happy, neither giving an inch. Downing whisky sours in the dining car, staring at each other in silence, then criticising, niggling, for all the world like two old married people falling out, and I guess our fellow travellers, or some of them, one old bird in particular with her *lorgnette* and pursed lips, were sure they knew how it was.

Then. Well, then it got better. Thanks to Robert. There at the Book–Cadillac he had a room for us on the twentieth floor. A sleazy little love-dump at twelve dollars a day, with a flea-ridden bed, and a gasping shower, and a view of back roofs and a water-tower. It was sleazy, sordid. But, somehow, it worked.

We flopped on the dumpling bed, and it sank like a badly made cake, and we both laughed, and then it was fun again, all clothes half off, and me on my knees on the threadbare carpet, and someone working a Hoover out in the passage, and whistling, and you muttering rude things in my ear, and I trying hard not to squeal with joy when you pulled my knickers down, and then lying moaning, smothered in kisses, and feeling safe again, if only for then, if only for a few hours.

Sure, Harry. You knew how to give a girl a good time. Then and now. But it didn't last. We quarrelled again. Finding some pretext out of the air, some fault in the way I spoke, or the way I did my hair, and I lashing back, at your clothes, or your family, or Caresse, or, worst of all, at your poetry and your games with the sun – that hurt the most, and

I knew it did. We were shouting, and throwing things, pillows at first, and then the soap, or the bedside Bible, or whatever else came to hand, until we were struggling, arm to arm, and it was fun again. I fought like a tiger, but let you take me, knock me around in a gently savage way, and then overpower me. God how I loved it when you used me like a whore, like a woman sprung upon in a dark alley, a chambermaid making a bed, a little virginal schoolgirl washing her breasts in the locker-room. We had such fantasies.

Later, we went out, into the dark and the cold, to a party, maybe, with Robert, where no one knew us, and there was black idol, and dim light, and strange people who danced cheek to cheek. We walked alongside the cars, watching the fire and smoke from the great automobile factories labouring on through the night, and the black polluted river, and then home, to our little dirty, high, exciting room.

One day we went up to Canada, and walked in the snow, and were arm in arm at the station, coming back, when I saw a girl I knew. Face to face there by the train, someone I went to school with, in her small feathered hat, with her wispy hair and her sly tongue, nodding, and then colouring, pretending to smile, pretending, the little bitch, that she hadn't seen our arms interlinked – and it was then that the idyll, if that's what it was, Harry, went suddenly dirty, very badly so.

I started to cry. And it didn't work, the dumpy bed, or your fingering hands, or the black idol, or whisky, or anything else. I went on crying. Into the night. Not knowing exactly why. But out of control. And you went out and booked a berth on the night train – the Wolverine – and you came back and packed the bags, while I cried, and ordered a taxi, and paid the bill. Somehow we got to the station, and into the sleeper, and up and on to the hard, shaking, dim-lit little bed, and there all night we lay in each other's arms, too close really for love, catapulted through snow and darkness, until I was no longer crying, and this was the worst and the best time we have ever had, but it felt like goodbye.

Back in New York, we said it was. I was sick as a cat —
from opium, or from crying, or whisky, or all three. I lay at
Mortimer's flat, and you said that it had to end, at least for a
while, I would have to go back to Albert, and you to
Caresse, and let things take a break, and I cried again. Then I
struck you, across the face, and we were at odds and
quarrelling worse than ever before, and there wasn't a way
we could see to come close enough to kiss, or make love. So
you left. And I lay alone, and then dried my eyes, and I left,
too.

I went to my bridesmaid's, to Margaret at her parents'
apartment on Park Avenue, and I stayed alone again as long
as I could, which wasn't long, Harry, just three days. Three
days ago. You thought I was back with Albert in Boston,
and you made the best you could of it with Caresse, that very
night you were with her, all night, at Hart's party for you in
Brooklyn, a slew of poets and literary men and very drunken
sailors – okay, Harry, I take your word. I know the score.
And I was alone.

Alone, and writing. For two long days I lay in bed, or
paced the apartment, eating next to nothing, saying I wasn't
well, having something brought up to my room, and
writing, Harry. Writing my poem. It's there now, in your
pocket, sure it is. My one and only real poem. My heart's
blood into words. My testament, and my gift. You got it the
morning Caresse had her telegram, from the Aviator 'MISS
YOU LOVE SICK'. That was dynamite, I guess.

I see you both yesterday, Harry, reading your private
letters. Hers short, yours long. But each one like a fire. I see
you pace around each other, then ask to see. Then refuse.
Then reach for them anyway. And read. So I broke her,
Harry. I guess I broke her apart, with Pamela. She could
hardly have ignored, or got over, our child. She wanted one,
and you never gave her that. I had something she never had,
and she knew. She knew, Harry. Now she knew. And you
knew, too. That the Aviator affair was real. It had love in it,

the bite of need. And the two of you were apart, and for ever now. Win or lose. Live or die.

So this morning you rose as usual, shaved, and put on your black tie, and bought a fresh black gardenia, and arranged to go out with Caresse to see Narcisse Noir, sculpted in black by your friend from Boston, at the Varra Gallery, and then you took off your spectacles to kiss her goodbye, and ate your lunch alone. You knew already what had to happen, and you caught a cab, and I was already here, chatting to Mortimer. And the clock was ticking, Harry. The clock still ticks. And the sand was in the glass and running. Running fast.

Twenty-Four

So here we are, Harry. Waiting. Waiting for the clock to chime seven and the bottle of Cutty Sark to run dry. Waiting for Hart with his theatre tickets, for your mother to finish doing her hair before dinner, for Caresse to put the last touch of scent into the slender cavity behind her ears, and adjust her stockings, and smile in the mirror, or try to, and wonder if she ought to come down the great hotel stairs and go through the evening ahead.

We're all waiting, Harry. And meanwhile, standing there at the window, dark as the night in your dark suit, and shaking the empty bottle, the last of life in the old Scotch, the old ship, you can only imagine what may become. What may in its own time (not yours any more, or mine) take place, and replace our flash in the sun in this bloodracked, awful century.

So we wait, Harry. I here on the bed fully dressed, except for my crocodile shoes, in my little party dress, with the orchid still at my shoulder, the pearls around my neck, and the hole, yes, Harry, the necessary and unignorable hole, still here like the place of generation, the doorway to Hades, in the alabaster skin of my head. I here. You there a few feet away, but at a distance, no human imagination can calculate by the short report of a shot. And in black already, the hangman's terrible black, Harry, the death-colour, the ready-made inexorable funeral clothes you were always wise enough to be wearing.

Kick your shoes off. Come and lie down beside me here. Black socks. Black trouser creases. Black lapels. Look at me, Harry. But not for too long. Not any more. It's time now. Time for the stubby, sun-barrelled pistol again in your hand, and the arm around my shoulder, the way you have it rehearsed, Harry, the way it will look so strange in the newspapers. A love suicide. A pact to die. A weird couple who went across the barrier hand in hand. Smiles on their faces, alcohol in their blood.

And Albert, the widower, Albert, the wronged husband, will never know, or never believe what he hears. Not even the letters. Not even the anonymous telephone calls. Not even the evidence of the Detroit Hotel bills in the book they will one day write about us, Harry.

Listen. Do you hear the clock chime in the belfry? The great cathedral ringing? I think I do. Or I would if I were alive. I would hear the water twist in the cistern there in the wall, a bird sing on the sill in the darkness, the little dirty feet of the last cockroach of summer clambering over the jerry-can below the bed. I would hear my own heart still beating out its message of love and time, I would hear the rasp of my breath, and the swish of my knickers every time I moved my thighs, I would hear the creak of my own ribs, and the gurgle of dinner and whisky troubling my stomach.

Never again. Never the smell of the tar in the road outside the house, never the faint aroma of coffee filtering into my dreams in the morning, or the stale dregs of wine sifting over my brain falling asleep after a wild party at night-time. Never the stench of my own wastes, Harry, the rich effluvia of being alive. Never the scent of soap, or the fine high stink of lotions.

So tell me. Who do you see? Who do you see in the black shape on the bed, the pretty girl with her skirt mussed, and her eyes open? The sweet available mistress you had and wanted, Harry, or someone else now? Not any more the young fine thing you adore. But another, Harry. The bent, strange figure you saw first those many years ago when your father told you off for throwing bombs from the Chinese room, the dark image in the drawing room, your first sight of death in the frame of your grandmother sewing. The same shape that was there when the ambulance went into splinters around your vulnerable flesh, and there was nothing but empty sky, and you and God, so you thought, and then all that you saw was an old woman lifting a long hood from her face, and you screamed, Harry. And that was your second sight.

Third time lucky. Sure. You don't always get a look at a corpse in such fine, prime condition as this, Harry. Before the salts of the morgue. In its neat, original wrapper, too. Dress fit for a queen. Jewels to please a lady. This is your bride, Harry. The real virgin girl you took to cross over the water with. Untouched in her first skin. Unbroken. Un-wavering. And already ahead of you. There. Tall, slight. On the other bank. With her hand in the air. Beckoning, Harry.

Take the gun. Check that the cartridge is there in the breech. Free the trigger. Compose your mind. And write something? No, Harry. It's all written already. Clear as daylight. In the monologue of your dreams, your thoughts about what to do now. Each word that I seem to say, Harry, the words you know you make me say – each delicate, wavering sentence bent in the air like a daffodil, each paragraph of disordered reason. It's your testament. It's your explanation. And, yes, Harry. It's there.

Never mind that the cub reporters who come through the axed door from the *Globe* won't be able to read it. Licking their pens and slanting cameras over the headboard. Never mind that the police inspector with his notebook and his rag for bloodstains won't ever hear what you have to say. Never mind that the state pathologist, with his bag and his rolled-up sleeves, and his clever knives and his bottle of formaldehyde, won't even know that the words are there in your very guts, in your brain, Harry, imprinted for all to see on the lines of your nerves.

They don't matter. Nothing matters. No one matters now. Not even your magical Jacqueline, with her heavy chin on her stick, and her feet as bare as mine. Only you matter, Harry. You and I. But then, you and I are the same now, the same as we always were. Only I could see it, Harry, how I could lead you along the path of your own destiny to this point where we merge as one, and go blind into the sun. The darkness. The place of origin and decay.

Make yourself comfortable. Remember your father. Your mother, Harry. They'll care. Oh, of course, they'll care. But they won't understand. They won't ever properly know what brought us to lie on this narrow bed smiling into each other's eyes, like a pair of Japanese dolls, too pretty to live. They'll go through their lives, Harry, and, sure, they'll always remember, but not what will happen tonight, what had happened already this afternoon, oh no, Harry, they'll go back to the sea sounding on Coffin Beach, and the games of golf you never won, and the sound of the whistle that used to bring you running, saying, 'Sir.'

And Caresse. She'll be there, too. Living on, growing old. Having her lovers, and never forgetting. Bringing your uncorrected remaining poems out, Harry, the ones that can never show how far you got when you lay here tonight in the long run down into what might seem profound, and explain the world, and still shock, and amuse, and fit your own mind, and be something no one else had ever done. You've done it, Harry. Taken the shape of your vision and made it your own. By a single blow. A strike. A shot from a gun.

Two shots. Oh yes, it takes two shots. There's no going down those stairs alive, handcuffed to some miserable oak with your face shattered like glass in the flash-bulbs, and your haggard smile across the front page, and your beautiful lonely body propped up in a box of mahogany to answer questions: 'Yes, my Lord, no my Lord, I mean I never meant to, I mean I did mean to, except that there wasn't time. I mean. Oh Christ, I don't know what I mean.'

And then to be dragged in shirt-sleeves to a wooden chair, with iron plates on your calves, and a bolt of current out of a steel machine that will break your ganglia into fragments, and maybe leave you alive still for a few seconds, a vegetable with a soul, and with no one to go with. Most important of all, Harry. No one to hold your hand, and to share your glory, and look in your eyes.

Put on the light. We need the light. Something for people to see us by. How many hours, I wonder, will we lie here? Gathering dust on our eyes. No one coming. No one knowing. Or knowing for sure.

You feel what will come, Harry. I see you do now. So take the gun in your fist. Arrange your fingers around the butt. It must seem to be properly done. Hold back about a foot from my face, and put the barrel to your own head.

I know. It feels cold. Very cold at one's temple. The moment before. The split second in front of the flash, and the peroration, the smack on the skin. What happens then? What happens, Harry? Tell us. Tell us if you ever can. Put words in my own mouth about that, if you will. But it's too late, you won't. No. Not ever now. You're squeezing the trigger. The mechanism is in motion. Nobody's left, Harry. Not even you or I. Are you touching me? Are your fingers moving on my skin? Or is it only the handful of insects in the skirting-board, and the wash on the walls, and the light shining on, and the echo, going away and away, and the short sharp smell of cordite, and a taste – oh, can I call it a taste, really? – of what was once a bottle of Cutty Sark, left floating like a resonance, a message launched in a bottle out to sea, for the whole future to follow, still in my mouth. Still in your mouth.

CROSBY DIED FOR A THRILL,
SAYS PARIS, JEERING 'PACT'

Chicago Tribune

POET SLEW SOCIETY SWEETHEART,
NO SUICIDE PACT

Daily Mirror

AN EROTIC EPIC OF TWISTED LIVES
ILLICIT LOVE AND HEARTS IN EXILE

Daily Mirror

Acknowledgments

In the course of researching Harry Crosby's life story I found the following works invaluable:

The Passionate Years by Caresse Crosby (Carbondale, Illinois: Southern Illinois University Press, 1968); Harry Crosby's *Shadows of the Sun* (Paris: Black Sun Press, 1928) also available in a more recent edition edited by Edward German, *Shadows of the Sun: Diaries* (Santa Barbara, Black Sparrow Press, 1977); his poetry: *Sonnets for Caresse, Red Skeletons, Transit of Venus, Mad Queen, Sleeping Together, Aphrodite in Flight: Being Some Observations on the Aerodynamics of Love*, all published by Black Sun Press; and his *Collected Poems* and *The War Letters*, also published by Black Sun Press. And, lastly, Geoffrey Wolff's very excellent biography of Harry Crosby, *Black Sun* (London: Hamish Hamilton, 1977).

Louise Erdrich
The Beet Queen £3.50

Long before they planted beets in Argus and built the highways, there was a railroad. Along the track, which crossed the Dakota–Minnesota border and stretched on to Minneapolis, everything that made the town arrived. All that diminished the town departed by that route, too. On a cold spring morning in 1932 the train brought both an addition and a subtraction. They came by freight. By the time they reached Argus their lips were violet and their feet were so numb that, when they jumped out of the boxcar, they stumbled and scraped their palms and knees through the cinders.

'Violent, passionate, surprising . . . small towns, the prairies, people trashed by circumstance, sexual obsession – all the matter of the classic American novel. *The Beet Queen* imparts its freshness of vision like an electric shock' ANGELA CARTER, THE GUARDIAN

'Erdrich is among our most powerful writers . . . she can weave a web as fine as any spider's, but hers is made of steel' MARTIN CRUZ SMITH, AUTHOR OF GORKY PARK

'She is a writer of formidable strength and imagination, and she presents the fruits of both in a prose of cold, flexible, haunting beauty' BERNARD LEVIN, SUNDAY TIMES

'I do not know anyone else writing about the things Louise Erdrich does. She's an original' GAIL GODWIN

'The range of her sympathy is astonishing . . . She shares with Faulkner the gift of transcending the mundane' PAUL BAILEY, OBSERVER

Lisa St Aubin de Terán
The Bay of Silence £2.95

Rosalind and William have all the appearance of success: a couple of beautiful people in their thirties, she an actress and he a graphic designer, revisiting Sestri Levante on the Italian Riviera where they once spent their honeymoon. But they have been driven there by paranoia — by a slow dread of what will happen to the two of them if anyone finds out about their baby Amadeo, whose identity, and even whose existence, is at the heart of the schizophrenia from which Rosalind has long suffered . . .

'She has the surrealist's gift for making the mundane exotic'
ISABEL QUIGLY, FINANCIAL TIMES

'I was rather shattered by it . . . it ends up a very macabre and fantastic book indeed, and I don't think I've really quite got over it yet'
VICTORIA GLENDINNING ON BBC RADIO 4'S KALEIDOSCOPE

'It draws, inevitably, parallels with *Tender is the Night* and, beside it, stands up as equal. It is a quiet yet astonishingly powerful and absorbing novel at the forefront of contemporary British fiction' BRITISH BOOK NEWS

'Compulsively readable and written with grace and a new authority which adds to the appeal of this most interesting author' COSMOPOLITAN

All these books are available at your local bookshop or newsagent, or can be ordered direct from the publisher. Indicate the number of copies required and fill in the form below.

Send to: **CS Department, Pan Books Ltd., P.O. Box 40, Basingstoke, Hants.   RG21 2YT.**

or phone: 0256 469551 (Ansaphone), quoting title, author and Credit Card number.

Please enclose a remittance* to the value of the cover price plus: 60p for the first book plus 30p per copy for each additional book ordered to a maximum charge of £2.40 to cover postage and packing.

*Payment may be made in sterling by UK personal cheque, postal order, sterling draft or international money order, made payable to Pan Books Ltd.

Alternatively by Barclaycard/Access:

Card No.

Signature:

Applicable only in the UK and Republic of Ireland.

While every effort is made to keep prices low, it is sometimes necessary to increase prices at short notice. Pan Books reserve the right to show on covers and charge new retail prices which may differ from those advertised in the text or elsewhere.

NAME AND ADDRESS IN BLOCK LETTERS PLEASE:

Name

Address

3/87